ACTION
ADRENALINE
ADVENTURE

D1333991

THIS WORLD BOOK DAY 2020
BOOK IS A GIFT FROM YOUR LOCAL
BOOKSELLER AND WALKER BOOKS

#SHAREASTORY

CELEBRATE STORIES. LOVE READING.

This book has been specially created and published to celebrate **World Book Day**. World Book Day is a charity funded by publishers and booksellers in the UK and Ireland. Our mission is to offer every child and young person the opportunity to read and love books by giving you the chance to have a book of your own. To find out more, and for loads of fun activities and reading recommendations to help you to keep reading, visit **worldbookday.com**

World Book Day in the UK and Ireland is also made possible by generous sponsorship from National Book Tokens and support from authors and illustrators.

World Book Day works in partnership with a number of charities, who are all working to encourage a love of reading for pleasure.

The National Literacy Trust is an independent charity that encourages children and young people to enjoy reading. Just 10 minutes of reading every day can make a big difference to how well you do at school and to how successful you could be in life. **literacytrust.org.uk**

The Reading Agency inspires people of all ages and backgrounds to read for pleasure and empowerment. They run the Summer Reading Challenge in partnership with libraries; they also support reading groups in schools and libraries all year round. Find out more and join your local library. **summerreadingchallenge.org.uk**

BookTrust is the UK's largest children's reading charity. Each year they reach 3.4 million children across the UK with books, resources and support to help develop a love of reading. **booktrust.org.uk**

World Book Day also facilitates fundraising for:

* **Book Aid International**, an international book donation and library development charity. Every year, they provide one million books to libraries and schools in communities where children would otherwise have little or no opportunity to read. **bookaid.org**

* **Read for Good**, who motivate children in schools to read for fun through its sponsored read, which thousands of schools run on World Book Day and throughout the year. The money raised provides new books and resident story-tellers in all the children's hospitals in the UK. **readforgood.org**

Titles by Anthony Horowitz

The Alex Rider series:
Stormbreaker
Point Blanc
Skeleton Key
Eagle Strike
Scorpia
Ark Angel
Snakehead
Crocodile Tears
Scorpia Rising
Russian Roulette
Never Say Die
Secret Weapon
Nightshade (coming April 2020)

The Power of Five (Book One): *Raven's Gate*
The Power of Five (Book Two): *Evil Star*
The Power of Five (Book Three): *Nightrise*
The Power of Five (Book Four): *Necropolis*
The Power of Five (Book Five): *Oblivion*

The Devil and his Boy
Granny
Groosham Grange
Return to Groosham Grange
The Switch
Scared to Death

The Diamond Brothers books:
The Falcon's Malteser
Public Enemy Number Two
South by South East
The French Confection
The Greek Who Stole Christmas
The Blurred Man
I Know What You Did Last Wednesday

ALEX RIDER
UNDERCOVER
FOUR SECRET FILES

ANTHONY HOROWITZ

WALKER
BOOKS

First published 2020 by Walker Books Ltd
87 Vauxhall Walk, London SE11 5HJ

2 4 6 8 10 9 7 5 3 1

This collection © 2020 Stormbreaker Productions Ltd
Individual stories © 2008, 2013, 2020 Stormbreaker Productions Ltd
Cover illustration © 2020 Walker Books Ltd
Trademarks Alex Rider™, Boy with Torch logo™
© 2020 Stormbreaker Productions Ltd

The right of Anthony Horowitz to be identified as author
of this work has been asserted by him in accordance
with the Copyright, Designs and Patents Act 1988

This book has been typeset in Officina Sans

Printed and bound in Germany by GGP Media GmbH

British Library Cataloguing in Publication Data:
a catalogue record for this book is
available from the British Library

ISBN 978-1-4063-9495-5

www.walker.co.uk

CONTENTS

INTRODUCTION

Have you ever thought about becoming a paid assassin?

Inside this book, you will find two stories about Yassen Gregorovich, the cold-blooded killer who turned up in quite a few of the Alex Rider books, including *Stormbreaker* and *Eagle Strike*. After you've read about him, you may decide that the life of an assassin is not for you and all in all this is probably a sensible decision. But I have to say, I loved writing about him. There's something very interesting about someone who has no morality, no sense of right or wrong, who will do anything for money. He reminds me a bit of my publisher. I even made him the hero of his own novel ... *Russian Roulette*. Do look for it in your school library and if it's not there let me know the name of your school librarian!

Metal Head, the story of a horrible school inspector, was written specially for this World Book Day edition and has never been published before. The story is set in Russia in 1990 or thereabouts ... in a very different world to the one we inhabit now. It might interest you to know that everything I write about Yassen's school is based on fact. Children in Russian schools wore uniforms and were given lessons in NVP – or military training – where they were taught how to handle machine guns. Anyway, I hope you enjoy the rather unusual twist at the end. It certainly made me smile.

The other story, The White Carnation, finds Yassen a little later in his career. Again, it has an unexpected ending. In a way it's a story about unhappiness but it's also about hope and about life. It originally appeared in an early edition of *Russian Roulette*, but unless you hunt around antique bookshops, you're unlikely to find it any-where else except here.

Double Agent tells the story of yet another assassination! Maybe *Undercover* is the wrong title for this book. *Undertaker* would have been better. It describes a terrible incident in Alex Rider's life, although he does not appear himself – he is only three months old. I wrote it as a sort of epilogue to the seventh Alex Rider novel, *Snakehead* (which is still one of my favourites). It introduced Alex's godfather, a man called Ash, and this is very much his story too. I think it's interesting to know what made Alex Alex. This fills in one of the gaps.

But an Alex Rider book, even a fairly short one, wouldn't be complete without an adventure starring

Alex himself and to begin this collection I wrote a brand new story, The Man with the Wrong Shoes. It takes place just after Alex gets back from France and his second mission ... to infiltrate the weird Point Blanc Academy, run by the sinister Dr Grief. If you've read the book, you'll remember that it ends with a fight at Alex's school in West London. This, if you like, is what happens next. I often wondered what the head teacher of Alex's school must have thought about all the strange things that were going on.

2020 is a landmark year for Alex Rider.

You may have noticed the silver flash on the cover of this book – it's a reminder that it is now twenty years since the first Alex Rider novel came out. I find it impossible to believe that so much time has gone by and it makes me quite angry to think that although Alex is still in his early teens, I've been getting older and older. Walker Books is publishing a special anniversary edition of *Stormbreaker* in February. Maybe they'll also buy me a cake.

April is even more exciting ... for me anyway. That's when the thirteenth Alex Rider book comes out. I'm not allowed to give too much away but it's called *Nightshade* and it takes place a few weeks after Alex has returned to school following his encounter with the vicious Grimaldi brothers in the South of France and in Wales. The new novel is set in the UK, Gibraltar and Crete and finishes with a devastating terrorist attack on London which only Alex can prevent. You can let me know what you think of it but I'm quietly optimistic. It's the longest Alex Rider book so far ... with the most action!

May sees the publication of the sixth graphic novel, *Ark Angel*, brilliantly adapted by Antony Johnston (sadly, someone stole the H in his first name) and illustrated by Amrit Birdi. In August, the paperback edition of *Secret Weapon* comes out and if you haven't read it yet I hope you'll check it out. The first story, Alex in Afghanistan, is one of the best I've written. At least, I think so.

Finally, news of Alex Rider the television series! We filmed the second novel, *Point Blanc*, starring Otto Farrant as Alex and Brenock O'Connor as his best friend, Tom. As I sit here writing this – it's still only October 2019 – I don't know if it's going to be on ITV or BBC, Netflix, Amazon or wherever but I'm pretty sure it will be somewhere. I've seen the first three episodes and I couldn't be happier. Otto is perfect as Alex. The series has a slightly darker, more adult feel than the books but it's still very close to what I wrote. I've only seen rough cuts of the ironing-board-snowboard scene but it looks fantastic.

So that's the world of Alex Rider. I feel a bit embarrassed that I've written the whole of this introduction and I've barely mentioned World Book Day, which is what this is really all about.

I'm delighted that Alex was invited to join this wonderful initiative which aims to put a book into the hands of every child and young person in the UK. I don't want to go on about how great reading is. If you've managed to get all the way to the end of this introduction you must be a pretty keen reader anyway. But I would like to mention how fantastic it is to own books. I have two or three thousand of them in my house and although I won't pretend I've read them all, at least not from cover to cover, I've found something valuable in every single one of them and when I see them sitting on the shelf, they feel almost like friends.

I can't imagine growing up without being surrounded by books and although this one is very small, I hope it will be the start of a collection and that one day, years from now, you will find it and remember how much you enjoyed it. That's the thing about books. They stay with you for life.

Anthony Horowitz

This story takes place after Point Blanc, *the second Alex Rider novel (very soon to be seen on TV), in which Alan Blunt and Mrs Jones sent Alex to investigate the sinister Point Blanc Academy high up in the French alps. They were puzzled by a series of unexplained deaths that seemed to be connected to the ultra-secret school.*

Alex uncovered a plot by the head teacher – Dr Grief – to take over the world using clones, perfect replicas of wealthy children. He managed to alert MI6, but had to come up with a dizzying plan in his attempts to escape.

By the time Alex got home he had missed several weeks of term and Brookland Comprehensive was closed for the spring holidays. He was summoned to see the head teacher, Henry Bray ... but actually the telephone call was a trick.

His own clone had lured him into a trap. At the end of the story, the two boys fought on the roof of the science laboratory while it was burning down all around them. The clone – Julius Grief – seemed to fall to his death.

Now read on...

THE MAN WITH THE WRONG SHOES

1

Henry Bray, the head teacher at Brookland, was puzzled.

It had been several months since a mysterious fire had burned down the science block that had once stood next to his office and, although there had been a complete investigation, the cause was still unknown. According to the experts from the fire department, the blaze had begun in a laboratory on the ground floor and, fed by some of the chemicals kept in storage, it had quickly spread upwards until the entire building had been destroyed. The following day, Bray had been shown round what remained of the laboratory and he had noticed a series of pockmarks in one of the walls. They looked suspiciously like bullet holes, although the leading firefighter had done her best to assure him that they were simply cracks caused by the intense heat.

He still had his doubts. What exactly had

happened here? Brookland had been closed down, locked and bolted for the school holidays. Although there had been less security that day than there was during term time, the caretaker – Mr Lee – had been in the grounds and he hadn't reported anything unusual. There had been just one visitor that morning and he had recognized him immediately.

Alex Rider.

According to the caretaker, Alex had been on his way to the head teacher's office but that was impossible. Henry Bray had been on holiday in the Yorkshire Dales at the time and certainly hadn't called Alex in for a meeting. So why had he come? There had to be a simple explanation but right now Bray couldn't think of one. What really troubled him was that it was Alex who was involved. If it had been any of the other seven hundred and fifty boys and girls who attended Brookland, he might have been able to put it out of his mind. But Alex Rider was different. Ever since his uncle had died in a car accident, nothing about the boy had made any sense.

Until then, Alex had been a fairly ordinary student, bright but not brilliant, excellent at sport, popular amongst his classmates. Henry Bray, who was married with two sons of his own, tried to know as much as he could about all the students at Brookland and understood that Alex had lost both of his parents when he was very young. He was looked after by a housekeeper with an odd name – Jack Starbright – who occasionally turned up to parents' evenings, always apologizing that his uncle, Ian Rider, couldn't come because he was abroad.

It must have been awful for Alex to lose his one surviving relative and Bray had given him as much support as he could, including, of course, time off from school. Bray was concerned – but had said nothing – when that time off turned into several weeks, and he had been completely understanding when Alex had finally shown up again. But then Alex had disappeared a second time and Bray had felt he had to file a report.

Jack Starbright had sent him a note from a Dr Alan Blunt at the Chelsea and Westminster Hospital explaining that Alex was suffering from post-traumatic stress and would be away from school for some time – and that should have been the end of it. But then the fire had happened. And Alex had been there.

There was something else that was even stranger.

Bernard Lee, the elderly caretaker, had sworn that he had seen Alex on the roof, fighting with another boy while the fire was raging below.

"I didn't know what to do," the caretaker explained. "They were having a go at each other, hammer and tongs. It was like they wanted to kill each other."

"Who was the other boy?" Bray demanded.

"It was Alex!"

"I know. You just told me that. Alex was on the roof. But who was he fighting?"

"He was fighting himself!"

"You mean he was on his own?"

"No! There were two of them! Two Alex Riders! They were fighting each other!"

The caretaker was well into his sixties. He liked to have a drink in the evening – though usually after six o'clock. Henry Bray had decided his story made no sense and that Mr Lee must have been drunk or asleep and dreaming.

Unfortunately, it didn't end there.

Other witnesses had seen the emergency services arrive. A teenage boy with short, fair hair and brown eyes had been loaded into the back of an ambulance ... and from what Bray had heard his description exactly matched Alex Rider. But when Bray met Alex a few days later, he was completely unharmed. He also denied having come anywhere near Brookland at the time of the fire.

It was a complete mystery.

In the end, Bray had written a letter outlining all his worries. He had sent one copy to the police commissioner in charge of the investigation and another to the local authority. He wasn't by nature a suspicious person and he had no wish to get Alex into trouble, but he was acutely aware that he was personally responsible for the safety of all the boys and girls who attended his school. If there was something sinister going on, he needed to know about it.

The letter that he had received back had been short and to the point.

> Dear Mr Bray,
>
> Thank you for your letter. The Brookland science block has now been examined by experts. The fire was caused by a gas leak which was sparked by static electricity in the carpets.
>
> We have no record of any boy being taken away by ambulance.
>
> We understand that the science block was covered by your insurance and can be rebuilt. We must point out that if you wish to open an investigation into what happened, it will delay any pay-out being made to Brookland School.
>
> It might be sensible, therefore, to consider this matter closed.
>
> Yours sincerely,
> John Crawley

The signature was difficult to read, little more than a dark blue scrawl. There was nothing in the letter to explain who exactly Mr Crawley was.

Henry Bray had no choice. The school couldn't operate without a science block and he needed to move forward as quickly as possible. Even so, he was surprised how soon the money arrived. Most of the insurance companies he'd dealt with did everything they could to avoid having to pay out.

This time, the money was in the Brookland account within days. Plans for the new block were drawn up. A construction company was found. The new building work had already begun.

The head teacher got up from his desk and went over to the window. The burnt-out science block had been covered in scaffolding and now stood in the middle of a construction site, surrounded by a tall wire fence with a single gate leading in and out, guarded around the clock. There were about a dozen workers in hi-vis, yellow vests and bright red helmets. An eighty-metre crane had somehow sprung up overnight and it was already lifting metal RSJ beams to strengthen the new roof. Bray looked out at the usual jumble of pipes and cables, cement mixers, wheelbarrows and the array of wood and plastic cabins – toilets, offices, storage – around the side. It was going to be difficult for the children to concentrate in school with all this activity going on. He couldn't wait for it to be over.

The telephone on his desk rang. He went over and picked it up.

"Mr Bray?"

Bray recognized the voice of the school secretary, Jane Bedfordshire. She was usually warm and friendly but right now she sounded anxious. "Yes, Miss Bedfordshire?"

"I've been asked to tell you that Jasper Milvain has arrived."

"I'll be right down."

Bray was wearing a suit and tie, but because of the warm weather he had taken off his jacket and hung it on the back of his chair. Reluctantly, he drew it on again. Right now, the very last thing he wanted to do was to meet the Right Honourable Jasper Milvain, Member of Parliament for West Brompton and Chelsea. Unfortunately, he had not been given any choice.

Jasper Milvain was a short, overweight man with slicked back hair and ruddy cheeks. He looked out on the world through thick spectacles, his eyes always blinking as if he was afraid of being found out. He had entered Parliament after a career in the law and had risen quickly through the ranks. At the last election, he had been made Junior Minister for Education.

The head teacher of Brookland School had plenty of reasons to dislike Jasper Milvain. It wasn't just the politician's appearance, the way he dominated any conversation. It was his policies. Milvain wanted to bring back corporal punishment, arguing that there was too little discipline in modern schools. He also had some interesting ideas about modern education. He thought drama, art and music were a complete waste of time and wanted them dropped from the curriculum. He was also against reading for pleasure. His speech at the last party conference had been widely reported in the press:

"Everyone always goes on about the value of books and libraries," he had said. "But actually,

I disagree. If children want to read *Harry Potter* or Michael Morpurgo at home with their parents, that's all for the better. But education should be about getting a good job and that means maths, science, engineering, economics and languages. If we want to prepare young people for the challenges of adult life, I'd say we need fewer libraries and more laboratories. That, ladies and gentlemen, is the future!"

Henry Bray disagreed with everything that Milvain stood for. Of course he knew the value of science but he had always supported reading. Brookland had a book club. Twice a week, students were sent home with books to read instead of homework. His one disappointment was that the school library had been badly designed with too many windows so that it was hot in the summer and chilly in the winter and never as welcoming as he would have liked. The roof had also leaked with the result that almost a hundred books had been damaged. After the science block had burned down he had secretly told his wife that he wished it had been the library. He would have welcomed the insurance money as an opportunity to rebuild the whole thing and start again.

Milvain had invited himself here for a photo-opportunity with the London press. It absolutely suited him – and his message – to be photographed in front of a brand new science block that was just in the process of being built. That afternoon, he was going to deliver a speech to the whole of Years Nine, Ten and Eleven. It didn't bother him that he had completely disrupted the school day. He would be on the six o'clock news and in all the newspapers the following day. He had also made it clear that when the new building was finished, he wanted to come back and officially open it. He had even suggested that it might be named after him.

The trouble was that Milvain was the local MP for the area. He was also powerful. If Bray had refused to allow him into the school, he might well have found that funding for Brookland had mysteriously dried up. His own future there might be called into question. He had allowed the other staff members to persuade him. It was only one hour. He just had to grit his teeth and try to put on his best smile.

Even so, as he made his way downstairs, Henry Bray was feeling a little sick. He hated being used, particularly by someone as opinionated as Jasper Milvain.

His earlier thoughts were no longer in his mind. He had completely forgotten about Alex Rider.

2

Like everyone else at Brookland that day, Alex was not looking forward to missing class in order to stand out in the schoolyard listening to some politician lecturing them from behind a microphone. Ever since MI6 had entered his life, he'd missed enough school anyway. First there had been his visit to Sayle Enterprises down in Cornwall and his encounter with the deadly Stormbreaker computers. And just when he thought it was all over, he had been packed off to France, pretending to be the son of a billionaire businessman called Sir David Friend. That had also been a near-death experience with Dr Grief, which had not ended well.

As he walked out of the dining hall following lunch, he felt a strong twinge of guilt. Nobody in the school knew what he had been going through in the past months, working – reluctantly – for MI6. That was the part of his new world that he most disliked, having to lie to his friends. Nor could he tell anyone that he was at least partly responsible for the destruction of the science block. Julius Grief had wanted to kill him and he would have cheerfully burned down the entire school to achieve his aim. Like it or not, it was Alex who had brought him here.

And now he was having to join three year groups to listen to some local politician boasting about his achievements. Alex was fed up with politics. It often seemed to him that if he was as noisy and rude as half the people he saw in Parliament, he would be thrown out of school without a second thought. He had seen Jasper Milvain on TV, angrily wagging his finger at a crowd of climate change protestors, absolutely convinced that he knew more than all the world's scientists. Alex wasn't looking forward to the afternoon.

"At least we're missing history." Tom Harris, his best friend at Brookland, must have been reading his mind. He had caught up with him in the corridor.

"I like history," Alex replied.

"It's all just wars and people killing each other and kings and queens. I mean, who cares if the Spanish Armada took place in 1688?"

"Actually, I think it was 1588."

"That's exactly my point! What difference does it make?"

Alex wasn't in the mood to argue and anyway, just then, they were interrupted by a tall, curly-haired man who was coming the other way, pushing between them. Alex had met him a couple of times. His name was Kevin Doyle – a supply teacher who had only been at Brookland a few months. He was working in the English department and had volunteered to direct the school play. This year it was going to be *Macbeth* and Tom had been cast as the porter.

Mr Doyle looked miserable, sweating in a jacket that was too warm for the weather and carrying a bulging backpack. He was obviously in a hurry but he still stopped and turned to the two boys.

"Harris! I hope you've learned your lines by now."

"I'm working on them, sir."

"For heaven's sake, Harris! You only have one scene!" He turned to Alex. "And I'm very disappointed in you, Rider. You didn't even audition!"

While the auditions had been taking place, Alex had been in France, being chased down the ski slopes by men on 700cc snowmobiles with built-in machine guns. But he didn't tell the teacher that. "Maybe next year," he said.

"If I'm here next year." Doyle took out a handkerchief and wiped his forehead. Then he continued on his way.

The two boys watched him go. "What's wrong with him?" Tom asked. "He looked scared to death."

"Maybe he's seen your acting," Alex said.

Half an hour later, over two hundred children streamed out of the school and took their places on one side of the schoolyard, facing the podium where Milvain would speak. When the politician addressed them, he would have his back to the library and the fenced-off, soon-to-be-rebuilt science block site would be right in front of him. The whole event could have been staged deliberately – and probably had been.

The politician was not outside yet. He was having a coffee with the head teacher. But half a dozen press journalists and a camera crew stood waiting. On the other side of the fence, construction workers were going about their business as if nothing unusual was happening. The crane was hoisting a short, steel girder up towards the roof. A couple of engineers were in discussion with the site foreman. The hammering of a pneumatic drill was occasionally erupting in short bursts somewhere inside. Two heavy-set security men stood on either side of the gate, watching the crowd carefully.

Alex joined his friends, standing in orderly lines, everyone dressed in their best school uniforms. Mr Bray had made an announcement at assembly the day before: no crooked ties, no shirts outside trousers, no trainers. Everyone had to look their best, not for Jasper Milvain but for the local press. At least the weather was good: the sun was shining and there was a light breeze.

The only thing still missing was the MP. He often behaved this way. The longer he kept people waiting, the more impressive his entrance would seem. Several Brookland teachers were standing in the yard, keeping an eye on things – but even they didn't complain when the students began to fidget and talk amongst themselves. They probably wanted the whole thing to be over too.

Alex would genuinely have preferred to be doing history. He glanced through the fence at the burnt-out building surrounded by scaffolding and thought, once again, of his final encounter with Julius Grief, the clone searching for him, his face twisted with anger, the gun, the flames. He felt uncomfortable being here. He just wanted to go home.

And then he saw something.

A man had come out of one of the plastic cabins on the edge of the construction site. He was dressed just like the other workers: blue overalls, a fluorescent vest, a brightly coloured helmet. If he had simply continued forward, Alex might not have noticed him. But he had hesitated, looking left and right, as if he was checking that he hadn't been seen – and that had made him stand out. A moment later he began walking, but now Alex had him in his sights and he noticed something else.

The man had the wrong shoes.

Alex had been on building sites before. In fact that was where his journey to the Point Blanc Academy had begun, coming up against two drug dealers near Putney Bridge. He knew that everyone on a building site had to wear safety boots with steel toe-caps and reinforced soles. The man who was making his way across the site, keeping his head low and trying not to be seen, was wearing ordinary loafers. What did it mean?

Just then a door opened in the side of the school and Jasper Milvain walked out next to the head teacher, Henry Bray. He had two protection officers with him and several advisers. He waved cheerfully to the crowd and climbed onto the platform in front of the library. Before he began speaking, he waited for the applause to stop, although in fact there was no applause. Perhaps he had imagined it.

"Good afternoon..." he said.

The man on the building site had disappeared. Alex had briefly glanced at the visiting politician and when he turned his head back there was no sign of him. And suddenly he knew that danger was close by. He didn't have much evidence: just the way the man had hesitated and the fact that he was wearing ordinary shoes. But if there was one thing that his uncle had taught him, it was that sometimes instinct was enough. The spies who hesitated, who waited for absolute proof before they took action, were easily recognized. They were the dead ones.

"Alex? What are you...?"

Tom called out to him but he was already too late. Alex had broken away from the crowd and was sprinting round the side of the yard towards the fence. He might be wrong. He might be making a fool of himself. But he was determined to find out what was going on.

3

He couldn't run through the gate. The two security guards would never let him pass between them. Alex had seen their type before: all muscle but not much brain. It would take him too long to explain why he was worried and anyway they wouldn't believe him. He still wasn't completely sure that he believed himself.

How was he to get in? The gate was impossible. The fence was too high. He glanced over his shoulder. Miss Bedfordshire, the school secretary, had seen him disappearing and was whispering something to Mr Bray as the two of them stood next to the podium. Would they send someone after him? The thought made him move all the faster, following the fence round, wondering if he could find another entrance. As he continued, he was aware of a large vehicle rumbling past him. A moment later it was right next to him and it wasn't just large, it was elephant-sized; a cement mixer truck with a massive steel mixing drum that was rotating slowly even as it moved forward on its six wheels. A ladder ran up to a platform next to the hopper, which was shaped like the lip of an oversized jug and would be tilted downwards to allow the cement to pour into the discharge chute.

Alex was already running before he had worked out exactly what he was going to do. The cement truck had overtaken him but it was still moving fairly slowly and in just half a dozen strides he was right next to it, reaching out to grab hold of the ladder. As his hand closed around one of the lower rungs, he was almost pulled off his feet but somehow he managed to cling on as he was lifted clear of the surface of the road. Gritting his teeth, he pulled himself upwards, climbing the ladder, unseen by the driver.

Once he was on top, he would be able to jump over the fence. That was the idea. But there was a problem. The ladder was on the wrong side of the truck and to position himself next to the fence he would actually have to stand on top of the mixing drum itself. That wouldn't be easy with the truck rumbling forward. But worse still, the drum was still rotating! Alex could actually hear the liquid cement slurping around inside. It was going to be like being on a treadmill in a gym. Alex would have to run sideways simply to keep still and if he missed his footing, he would be thrown back down onto the road. He might break his neck. Or he might be swept underneath one of the giant wheels and crushed.

He reached the top of the ladder and stood on the platform. Once again, he glanced back. Everyone was watching Milvain, who was well into his speech. Nobody was looking at him. Meanwhile, the truck had almost reached the end of the fence. If Alex was going to act, he had just seconds in which to do it. This was the tricky part ... the do or die moment. Taking a breath, he stepped off the platform and onto the revolving drum. Now he had to time everything perfectly. He could feel the metal surface sliding away beneath his feet, threatening to drag him backwards to his death. Judging the exact speed, he half-walked, half-ran in the opposite direction, keeping himself in the same position. The fence was on the other side, about two metres away. He estimated that he was about seven metres up, about the height of a classroom. The ground on the other side was rough, covered with gravel. Get this wrong and all he would have managed to achieve was a broken leg.

He felt his feet leave the drum as he leapt forward. For a second, he was suspended in mid-air above the fence and he was terrified he was going to come crashing down on the wrong side. But his momentum had carried him forward. He had made it over! Now the training he had received from MI6 took over. Before they had sent him to Sayle Enterprises, they had shown him how to make a parachute jump. In fact, the jump had been cancelled but he still knew how to land.

It was a technique known as a PLF – a parachute landing fall. His feet and knees were together as he plunged down the length of the fence. As soon as he came into contact with the ground, he allowed his body to buckle, absorbing some of the impact. At the same time, he fell sideways onto his arm and shoulder, rolling over in the dirt. It still hurt him. All the bones in his body jolted against each other and the breath was forced out of him as if he had been punched in the stomach. But when he got to his feet a moment later, he was still in one piece. His jacket was torn and his elbow was burning. But nothing seemed to be broken.

There was no sign of the man with the wrong shoes.

Alex scurried across to a pile of oil drums and crouched down behind them, keeping out of sight while he caught his breath. He was lucky that nobody had seen him land in the building site. He knew that the moment anyone on the site noticed him he would be frog-marched back to school and quite possibly arrested. In the distance, he could see Jasper Milvain at the podium. He had obviously just made some sort of joke because he was smiling, pleased with himself. Alex looked from one construction worker to another and saw that he had a problem. Everyone was dressed the same. They all wore protective helmets. Some even had goggles.

The man that he was looking for could be any one of them and with so much equipment lying about the place, he couldn't even see all their shoes.

The man had gone. The whole thing had been a waste of time.

But then Alex remembered how this had all begun. It was the way that the intruder had emerged from a plastic cabin that had alerted him in the first place. He had definitely been doing something suspicious. He hadn't wanted to be seen. So what was it? What had happened inside?

Alex had no choice. He rose up and sprinted across the open ground, hoping that the building work and the visiting politician would keep everyone looking the other way. He was lucky. He reached the edge of the cabin – a blue, plastic rectangle about the size of a container on a ship. It had a door and a single window but a blind had been drawn down, preventing him from looking in. He tried the door. It was open. He went inside.

He was in a rough office made up of a trestle table covered with charts and diagrams, a folding chair, and a filing cabinet with a jug of water, an open can of Coke, a safety helmet and an ashtray jumbled next to each other on the top. At first he thought the office was empty. Then he saw the legs sticking out from underneath the table. With a sick feeling in his stomach, he hurried forward and knelt down beside the man who was stretched out on the floor, a pool of blood around his head. The man was in his forties. He had a moustache and a tattoo of a dragon on the side of his neck. There was an ugly gash in his forehead and this was where the trail of blood began. Alex noticed a monkey wrench lying on the floor beside him. It was easy enough to put the pieces together. The man had come into the office for a break. He had taken off his safety helmet and opened a Coke. Then someone had come in and hit him hard with a heavy duty, metal wrench that must have weighed a kilogram. The man might have fractured skull. He might be dead.

But then Alex saw the rise and fall of his chest. The man was still breathing. He reached up for the jug of water and poured some of it on the man's face. His eyes flickered and opened but otherwise he didn't move.

"What happened?" Alex demanded.

"Who are you...?" The man couldn't focus his eyes.

"Do you know who it was who hit you?"

"No. Never saw him before. Came in..." The man swallowed hard. Even talking was an effort.

"I'll get someone to come and look at you. But I need to know. Do you have any idea where he went?"

The man tried to shake his head but any movement caused him fresh waves of pain.

Alex was about to give up and fetch help. Then he had one last thought. "What do you do on the building site?" he asked.

"The crane..."

"What?"

"Operate ... the crane."

"I'll be right back!"

The man – the crane operator – would be OK. He wasn't in any danger. But now Alex knew that his instinct had been right. Here was the proof of it, lying semi-conscious on the cabin floor. There had been an intruder and he was dangerous. He had already badly hurt one man and he might well be intending to kill another. He had to be here because of Jasper Milvain. What other reason could there be? Another question sprang into Alex's mind. What could the intruder do if he took possession of the crane?

The answer was ... plenty.

Alex burst out into the open air and this time a construction worker saw him immediately.

"What the hell are you doing here?"

Alex ignored him, running back to the oil drums. From here he had a good view of both the school on one side and the crane on the other. He was too late! He could see a man sitting high above him in the compartment at the top of the crane. He was manipulating the controls. Quite deliberately, he lowered a second steel girder so that it was resting on the roof of the science block. It was quite short – no more than five or six metres. But it was solid and thick and Alex knew that if it fell on someone it would crush them, shattering every bone.

Was that the plan? To drop it on the junior minister?

But the girder was resting on the roof. Even as Alex watched, the operator released a length of the cable that ran from the girder to the end of the crane's arm. The cable was loose now, no longer bearing the weight of the load. What was he doing?

Alex saw the tiny figure – in the cabin high above him – reach for a lever and at once the arm of the crane began to swing towards the school. And at that moment he understood exactly what was being planned. He also knew that he had less than a minute to act.

The new crane operator was going to rotate the crane until the cable became taut again. When that happened, it would drag the girder off the top of the roof but by then, the arm of the crane would be some distance away. This would give it the momentum of a pendulum. When the girder, weighing a few hundred kilograms, came free, it would swing through the air like a deadly battering ram. It would miss the crowd of schoolkids – they were over to one side. Instead, it would break through the fence and continue forward in a straight line along the edge of the schoolyard, until – assuming the operator had aimed correctly – it slammed into the podium. The Right Honourable Jasper Milvain, Junior Minister in the Department of Education, would be smashed to pieces. In about fifty seconds time, the only way anyone would be able to recognize him was by his DNA.

Once again Alex was on his feet. He was aware

of the movement of the crane out of the corner of his eye but there was nothing he could do to stop it. He had to cover about one hundred metres. But he also had to make his way between two security guards and run the full length of the schoolyard. Before he could reach Milvain he had to deal with his entourage, his security officers and assistants. It was almost certain one of them would stop him if they saw him coming.

He was pounding through the construction site, heading away from the ruined science block and back towards the schoolyard. He heard someone shout out to him but he had no intention of stopping. The arm of the crane seemed to be following him. He risked the briefest glance behind him and saw the cable straightening out again. All too soon, it would drag the girder off the roof, turning it into a guided missile which would swing gleefully through the air before it found its target.

He reached the gate. Fortunately, the two burly security guards had their backs to him. Their job was to prevent anyone entering the building site rather than stop anyone coming out. However, one of them must have heard Alex's footsteps on the gravel. At the last moment, he turned and reached out to grab him. Alex had no choice. He couldn't stop now. He used a single elbow strike – a move he had learned in karate – to send the man reeling backwards, his arm completely numb. He had done no lasting damage. But now the way ahead was clear.

"I hope you will all make use of the wonderful science block that is being constructed here." Alex could barely hear Milvain's voice above the sound of his own tortured breathing. He didn't dare turn round but he could imagine the mass of steel swinging past him, finding its target. "It just remains for me to say..."

The entire crowd, two hundred students from Brookland, saw Alex racing across the yard towards the politician. One of them began cheering and immediately Milvain's voice was drowned out as the rest of them joined in. The teachers looked alarmed. Alex had almost reached the podium. One of the security men reached into his jacket. It was only now that Alex realized that he was probably armed.

A shadow fell across Alex's face. It was as if a plane had passed overhead. Only it wasn't a plane. It was the girder. It had been dragged off the roof and it had begun its deadly arc, propelled by the arm of the crane.

Alex reached the podium. Someone tried to stop him but he pushed them out of the way, then hurled himself at Milvain, bringing him down in a vicious rugby tackle. His shoulder, which he had already hurt leaping off the concrete truck, screamed at him. He felt something huge swing past and for a moment the light disappeared. Then he was on the floor, tangled up with the junior minister. He heard an explosion of shattering glass and metal followed by a terrible creaking and then more splintering and crashing as the entire building behind them collapsed in on itself. The girder had missed the politician – and Alex – by inches. But it had continued into the library.

When Alex looked up, the library was no longer there.

4

There were six people in Henry Bray's study. The head teacher was behind his desk. Alex was sitting on a chair to one side. On the other side of the room, handcuffed between two policemen, a man stood with his head lowered in shame. He hadn't spoken since he had climbed back down from the crane. The sixth person had been sent by Special Branch. Alex hadn't been told his name.

Bray turned to the man in handcuffs. "What were you thinking of, Mr Doyle?" he asked.

At the end of the day, Alex hadn't been too surprised that it was Kevin Doyle who had tried to kill the politician. He remembered meeting the supply teacher in the corridor. He had been sweating – not because it was hot but because he was thinking about what he was going to do.

Doyle turned slowly and glared at Alex. "You shouldn't have stopped me," he snarled. "People like him are ruining this country for people like us.

No books? No art? No drama? He makes the law but he knows nothing about education." He half-smiled. "Well, I was going to teach him a lesson."

Bray sighed. It was a cue for the man from Special Branch. "All right. Let's get him out of here," he said.

They left, taking their prisoner with them.

Alex was alone with the head teacher.

"I don't really know what to say, Alex," Bray began. "What were you doing on the construction site?"

"I just wanted to look at the new building," Alex said. "I sneaked in – and then I saw Mr Doyle operating the crane and I guessed what he was going to do."

"You do realize you were trespassing. You had absolutely no right to be there. And you could have been seriously hurt." Bray examined the boy with his torn jacket and his hair covered in dust. He sighed. "All in all, given what's happened, I think it's better if we say no more about it. The press have been told that the whole thing was an accident and we're making sure your name is kept out of it. And I'm happy to tell you that at least one good thing has come out of all this. The insurance will pay for the damage and so we'll be able to get a new library after all." He smiled to himself. "Do you think we should ask Jasper Milvain to open it?"

"No, sir."

"No. I don't think so either. Well done, Alex."

"Thank you, sir."

Nobody had thanked him for saving the politician's life but he supposed that was the way it was with modern politics. With a shrug of his shoulders, Alex turned and left.

DOUBLE AGENT

DOUBLE AGENT

The airport belonged to another age, a time when air travel was an adventure, when planes still had propellers and had to stop at strange-sounding places to refuel on their way across the world. There was just one runway, a narrow strip of silver-grey concrete cutting through grass that had been perfectly mown. The single terminal was a white building with a curving entrance and a terrace where people could watch the planes take off. It could have been the clubhouse of an expensive golf course.

The airport had no name. Although it was only an hour outside London, there were no road signs pointing to it. Indeed, it seemed to have done its best to lose itself in a maze of country lanes that looped and twisted through thick woodland. The local residents – and the nearest house was more than a mile away – believed it was a private flying club, used by millionaires with their own planes. For a brief time, it had been.

The airport had been bought by the British secret service back in the seventies, and now it was used for flights that nobody talked about. People who weren't meant to be in the country arrived here on planes that didn't exist. There was no passport control, because very few of the travellers carried passports – and if they did, they would probably be fake. A white control tower stood at the far end of the runway. It managed not just the incoming and outgoing flights but all the surrounding airspace. When planes were ready to take off here, Heathrow and Gatwick just had to wait.

At nine thirty on a cold morning at the end of April, a blue Rover Vitesse was making its way towards the secret airport. The sound of the V8 engine was almost inaudible as it cruised through a virtual tunnel of leaves. The start of the month had been warm and sunny, but there had been a cold snap the night before, and the result was a layer of fog floating over the ground deadening everything and turning the world a ghostly white. A man and woman were sitting in the back.

The driver had no idea who they were. His name was Enderby and he was a low-level MI6 operative trained for certain duties – the first of which was never to ask questions. He had picked them up at a London hotel at six o'clock exactly, loaded a single suitcase into the boot and brought them here.

And yet, glancing in the rear-view mirror, Enderby couldn't stop himself wondering about his passengers.

He guessed they were husband and wife. There was something about their body language that said as much, even though neither of them had uttered a word throughout the journey. The man was in his thirties, well built with close-cropped fair hair and dark, tired eyes. He was wearing a suit with an open-necked shirt. What would you think he was, seeing him in the street? Something in the City, perhaps. Private security. Ex-army. This was a man who knew how to look after himself. He had the relaxed confidence of someone who is very dangerous.

The woman sitting next to him was unhappy – Enderby had noticed that from the moment she had stepped reluctantly into the car. He could see it now in her eyes. They were nice eyes: blue, very bright. But they were troubled. All in all, she was very attractive. A couple of years younger than the man, maybe an actress or a dancer. She was wearing a jacket and grey trousers and – yes, there it was – a wedding ring on her finger.

Enderby was right. The two people in the back of his car were called John and Helen Rider. They had been married for four years. They were here because they were leaving the country – perhaps permanently. They had been apart for a long time, but that was all over now. Their new life together was about to begin.

They had almost arrived. Enderby had driven this route many times and recognized the elm tree with the nesting box hanging from one of its branches.

The airport was half a mile away. However, he was completely unaware of the advanced high-resolution camera with its 25mm varifocal lens concealed inside the nesting box. And he would have been surprised to learn that even now his face was being examined on a television screen inside the control tower. It was actually the third hidden camera they had passed in the last five minutes.

The car broke out of the wood and crossed a cattle grid set in the road. If the driver had been identified as an enemy agent, the grid would have rotated and shredded the tyres. The airport lay ahead; a plane was waiting on the runway. It was an old twin-engine Avro Anson C19 that might have been rolled out of a museum. Once used by the RAF for coastal patrol, the Anson hadn't been seen in regular service for twenty years. Certainly it suited the airport. They were both relics of the past.

A slim, dark-haired man stepped out of the terminal building, supporting himself on a heavy walking stick. He had been sent to supervise the departure. Enderby recognized him with surprise. He had visited the man a couple of times recently in hospital and had worked with him in the past. His name was Anthony Howell. His middle name was Sean.

People called him Ash.

The car slowed down and stopped. The man got out, went round and opened the door for the woman. The two of them moved forward to meet Ash.

"John. Helen." Ash smiled at them but he had recently been in a lot of pain. It still showed.

"How are you, Ash?" John Rider asked.

"I'm OK."

That obviously wasn't true. Ash was feverish, sweating. His hand was gripping the walking stick so tightly that the knuckles were white.

"You look terrible."

"Yeah." Ash didn't disagree. "They sent me to say goodbye. Are you ready? I'll get your case loaded on board."

He limped past them, over to the car. Enderby unlocked the boot and took out the suitcase.

"He's not very talkative," Helen muttered.

"He's hurt." John glanced at his wife. "Are you OK?"

"I don't like leaving Alex."

"I know that. Nor do I. But we didn't have any choice. You heard what the doctor said."

Alex Rider was three months old. Just a few days before, he had developed an ear infection which meant that he couldn't fly. Helen had left him with a cheerful Irishwoman, Maud Kelly, a maternity nurse who had been with them since the birth. Helen's first instinct had been to stay with her infant son. But she also needed to be with her husband. The two of them had been apart for too long.

"Maud will come out with him next week," John Rider said.

"His new home." Helen smiled, but a little sadly.

"It's strange to think he'll grow up speaking French."

"With a dad who's a fisherman."

"Better a fisherman than a spy."

Secret agents don't often retire. Some are killed in action; some leave the field and end up behind a desk, providing support for the men and women who have taken their place. Even when they leave the service, they are still watched – just in case they decide to sell their secrets or go into business for themselves.

John Rider was different. He had recently completed a long and brutal assignment which had culminated in a shoot-out on the island of Malta, followed by his faked death on Albert Bridge in London. During that time, he had inflicted serious damage on the criminal organization known as Scorpia. If Scorpia discovered that he was still alive, they would make him a primary target. MI6 knew that. They understood that his usefulness was effectively over. They had decided to let him go.

Ash came back over to them. He had a mobile phone in his hand. "The control tower just called," he said. "You're all set for take-off."

"Why don't you come and stay with us, Ash?" Helen suggested. "You could fly down with Alex. A week in the sun would do you good."

Ash tried to smile but something prevented him. "That's kind of you, Helen. Maybe..."

"Well, keep in touch," John Rider was examining

the other man with a certain unease. The two of them had worked together, but they had also been friends for many years.

"Good luck." Ash seemed in a hurry to get away. They shook hands. Then Ash leant forward and kissed Helen once on the cheek, but so lightly that she barely felt his lips. The husband and wife began to walk towards the plane.

"What's wrong with him?" Helen asked as soon as they were out of earshot. "I know he's hurt. But he seems so ... distant."

"He's been axed." John spoke the words casually. "He screwed up in Malta and he knows it. Blunt wants him out."

"What will happen to him?"

"An officer job somewhere. A junior outpost."

"Does he blame you?"

"I don't know, Helen. To be honest, I don't really care. It's not my business any more."

They had reached the plane. The pilot saw them through the cockpit window and raised a hand in greeting. His name was Robert Fleming and he had flown with the RAF in the Falklands war. Killing Argentine soldiers, some of them just kids, had changed his mind about active service; and after that he had allowed himself to be recruited by MI6. Now he flew all over the world for them. The co-pilot was a man called Blakeway. Both of them were married. There was no cabin crew.

Standing on the terrace outside the terminal,

Ash watched John and Helen Rider climb the metal staircase that led up to the plane. John stood aside to let Helen go first, gently taking her arm as she pulled the door shut from inside. A couple of ground crew in white overalls wheeled the steps away. The first of the Anson's two propellers began to turn.

Ash thought he was going to faint. The pain in his stomach was worse than ever. It was as if the Russian assassin Yassen Gregorovich had somehow managed to stab him a second time and was twisting the knife even now. The plane's engines had both started up but he could barely hear the sound. The sky, the grass, the airport, the Anson ... nothing connected any more. He could feel beads of sweat on his forehead. They were ice-cold. Could he really do this?

Was he going to go through with it?

He had been released from hospital after six weeks of treatment that had included being given eleven pints of blood. The doctors had told him what he already knew. He would never be the same again. Not completely. There had been too much damage. And the pain would always be with him. He would need a barrage of drugs to keep it at bay.

And had they been grateful, the people he worked for, the ones who had caused this to happen to him? He still remembered his meeting with Alan Blunt. The head of MI6 Special Operations had given him precisely five minutes: his injuries were his own fault. He had totally mishandled the operation in Mdina. He had disobeyed orders. He was being taken off active duty with immediate effect. Blunt hadn't even asked how he was feeling.

Ash had known what he was going to do even before he left Blunt's office. For a moment, the pain was forgotten; he felt only anger and disbelief. How could they treat him like this? No. It was obvious now. They had always treated him like this. Nothing had changed. He had been overlooked and underrated from the start.

But he had numbers. He had contacts. He didn't care what he had to do. He would show MI6 that they were wrong about him. They had made a mistake they were going to regret.

He made the call as soon as he was in the street, away from the eavesdropping devices that were scattered all over Special Ops HQ. After that, things happened very quickly. That same evening, he met a man in a south London pub. The next day, he was interviewed at length by two blank-faced men in an abandoned warehouse near the old meat market at Smithfield in Clerkenwell. Patiently he repeated everything he had said the night before.

The next call came two days later. Ash was given twenty minutes to get across London to the Ritz Hotel and a suite on the second floor. He arrived at exactly the specified time, knowing that he had almost certainly been followed the whole way and that it had been arranged like this to prevent him communicating with anyone else. There was to be no chance of a trap.

After he had been thoroughly searched by the two men he had met before, he was shown into the suite. A woman was waiting for him, sitting on her own in an armchair, her perfectly manicured fingers curving round a flute of champagne. She was strikingly beautiful with shoulder-length black hair and glittering, cruel eyes. She was wearing a designer dress – a whisper of red silk – diamond earrings and a single large diamond at her throat.

Ash tried not to show any emotion. But he knew the woman. He had never met her but he had seen her file. It was hard to believe that he was actually in the same room as her.

Julia Rothman.

According to the file, she was the daughter of Welsh nationalists, who had married – and murdered – an elderly property developer for his wealth. She was on the executive board of Scorpia. Indeed, she was one of its founding members.

"You want to join us," she said, and he heard a hint of Welsh in her voice. She seemed amused.

"Yes."

"What makes you think we'd be interested in you?"

"If you weren't interested in me, you wouldn't be here."

That made her smile. "How do I know we can trust you?"

"Mrs Rothman..." Ash wondered if he should have used her name. He spoke slowly. He knew he would only have this one chance. "I've spent four years with MI6. They've given me nothing. Now I've finished with them – or perhaps I should say they've finished with me. But you probably know that already. Scorpia always did have a reputation for being well informed. How do you know you can trust me? Only time will give you an answer to that. But I can be useful to you. A double agent. Think about it. You want someone inside Special Operations. That can be me."

Julia Rothman sipped her champagne but her eyes never left Ash. "This could be a trick," she said.

"Then let me prove myself."

"Of course. Anyone who joins Scorpia has to prove themselves to our complete satisfaction, Mr Howell. But I warn you: the task might not be an easy one."

"I'm ready for anything."

"Would you kill for us?"

Ash shrugged. "I've killed before."

"Before it was duty. For queen and country. This time it would be murder."

"I've already explained: I want to join Scorpia. I don't care what I do."

"We'll see." She set the glass down, then produced a white envelope. She slid it towards him.

"There is a man inside this envelope," she said.

"It is the name of a man who has done us a great deal of harm. Killing him will prove beyond all doubt that you mean what you say. But a warning. Once you open that envelope, you will have committed yourself. You cannot change your mind. If you try to do so, you will be dead before you leave this hotel."

"I understand." Ash was uneasy. He picked up the envelope and held it in front of him.

"We will provide the manner of his death," Mrs Rothman went on, "but you will be the one who pulls the trigger. And when he is dead, you will be paid one thousand pounds. It will be the first payment of many. Over the years, if you stay true to us, Scorpia will make you very rich."

"Thank you." Suddenly Ash's mouth was dry. The envelope was still balanced on his fingertips.

"So are you going to open it?"

He made his decision. He ripped the envelope open with his thumb. And there was the name in front of him. Black letters on white paper.

Julia Rothman looked at him quizzically.

So they knew. That was his first thought. The elaborate trick that had been played on Albert Bridge hadn't worked – or if it had, there had somehow been a leak. They had learnt that John Rider was still alive. And as for this test, they knew exactly what they were doing. Ash would have been happy to kill anybody in the world. He would have killed Blunt or anyone else in MI6. But Scorpia had gone one better.

They were asking him to kill his best friend.

"John Rider..." His mouth had gone dry. "But he's—"

"Don't tell us that he's dead, Mr Howell. We know he is not."

"But why...?"

"You said you didn't care what you did. This is your assignment. If you want to prove yourself to us, this is what you have to do."

But could he do it? He asked himself again now, watching the ancient plane as it completed the final checks before take off. The propellers were buzzing loudly; the whole fuselage was vibrating. And it wasn't just John. It was Helen Rider too. He had once loved her – or thought he had. She had rejected him. But John had always stood by him. No. That wasn't true. Blunt had axed him and John had done nothing to help.

The plane jerked forward and began to rumble down the runway, picking up speed.

The bomb was on board. Ash had no idea how Scorpia had got it there, or even how they had found out about the flight in the first place. Such details didn't matter. The fact was that it was there, and the cruelty of it was that Scorpia could easily have detonated it without his help. The bomb could have had a timer. They could have transmitted the signal themselves. But they had turned this into the ultimate test. If he did this, there would be no going back. He would be theirs for life.

We will provide the manner of his death, but you will be the one who pulls the trigger.

He couldn't do it. They were his closest friends. He was the godfather of their child.

He had to do it. John and Helen were dead anyway. And Scorpia would kill him if he failed.

The plane was halfway down the runway. Slowly it rose into the air.

Ash took out his mobile phone and pressed a three-digit number, followed by send.

The explosion was huge, much bigger than he had expected. For a moment, the plane disappeared completely, replaced by a scarlet fireball that hovered fifteen metres above the runway. There were no wings, no propellers, no wheels. Only flames. And then, like some hideous fireworks, broken pieces of glass and metal burst out of the inferno, bouncing off the tarmac and slamming into the lawn.

The plane had gone. There was nothing left of it. The people inside would have died instantly.

Already alarms were sounding. Enderby and half a dozen men were running towards the wreckage, coming from every direction – as if there was anything they could do. Black smoke billowed into the sky.

Ash turned away and walked back inside. He was sure that Scorpia would be watching. They would know that he had done it. He had passed the test. He took a deep breath and tasted smoke and burning aviation fuel.

A new life. But how was he going to enjoy it when he was empty inside? Too late. He had made his choice.

Slowly he made his way down the stairs and out onto the runway, limping towards the flames that for him would never die.

METAL HEAD

It's strange. When I was a schoolboy, I never dreamed that one day I would become a professional assassin, paid as much as two hundred and fifty thousand pounds a time to take the lives of people I had never met.

But when you're at school, you never really know what you are going to do when you are "grown up". Of course, there are some children who have a vision. They are going to be an artist, or a footballer, or a movie star or a millionaire. They talk about nothing else and the teachers like them because they are so ambitious. You never find out what happens to them after you go your separate ways. Some of them succeed. Some of them forget what it was that they wanted to do and they end up in different jobs and it may well be that they are perfectly happy.

I always wanted to be a helicopter pilot. I used to cut pictures out of magazines and pin them to the walls in my bedroom. I was fascinated by these huge machines, sitting on the ground like over-weight cows. How could they possibly rise up in the air with just two slim blades spinning crazily above them? When you look at a plane, you can imagine how it operates. A plane – if it's a glider – doesn't even need an engine. The wings do all the work. But a helicopter has no wings. It is ridiculous. When I was eleven years old, I imagined myself sitting in the cockpit of a Kamov Ka-22 Helix naval helicop-ter. Somehow I would have learned all its secrets. I would know which buttons to press and which levers to pull and I would make this great hunk of metal (it weighed six thousand kilograms) obey me.

And what would I do then? I didn't want to join the army or the air force. I had no interest in warfare. On the contrary, my ambition was to join Air Sea Rescue. I had seen them on television, these extraordinary men and women who, with no thought of their own safety, would swoop out of the sky when ships sank or when people were lost at sea. I would stare at the screen as they hovered, just a few metres above the crashing waves. How could they keep the helicopter – and their nerves – steady while the winch was lowered and some poor soul was plucked out of the freezing water? How did they feel as finally they soared back into the clouds, carrying their patients to the nearest hos-pital? To me, they were not just heroes. They were almost like gods.

I dreamed of becoming one of them. But things did not happen that way. I have saved very few people in my life. And if you were to take all the people whose lives I have destroyed, I can tell you this. You would not be able to fit them all into a helicopter. There would be too many of them.

I do not think I am an evil man. I do not take pleasure in what I do and the truth is that I might never have done it. I might indeed have become a pilot, but for the intervention of one man. His name was Igor Krokov, but I always knew him as Metal Head. Many people have helped to shape my life – but he was certainly the first.

Before I continue, I must explain something. The world that I am about to describe is not one that you may recognize. I am not talking about England or America or anywhere in the West. And the time I am referring to is not the time in which you live. I was brought up many years ago, back in the 1980s, in a little village called Estrov in what was then the USSR (the Union of Soviet Socialist Republics). Today, the country is known as Russia.

Some of what I am about to describe may sound very strange to you but at the end of the day, nothing very much has changed. Children are children. They crawl unwillingly out of bed and their parents shout at them to clean their teeth, to eat their breakfast, to hurry up and not be late for school. They work hard and they sit exams which fill them with terror. The future – adulthood – looks very far away and, to be honest, it's not all that attractive. Much better to enjoy the long summers with our friends, to go on bike rides, to get into trouble than to have to go to work every day and earn a living. At least, that was how it was for me.

I was thirteen years old and a student at the Alexander Blok School, named (in case you're wondering) after a famous poet. It was a big, ugly, red-brick building rising up three floors and every single classroom looked identical: the same size, the same colour, the same number of windows. The only difference was the pictures on the walls. So, in the chemistry classroom, there was a periodic table with all the elements. In the geography room, there were maps. In the history room, portraits of famous soldiers and politicians ... all of them Russian, of course. We were taught very little about the outside world.

My name, incidentally, was Yasha Gregorovich. Later on, I would become known as Yassen Gregorovich. But that, as they say, is another story.

I never had any difficulties at school. I worked hard. I did well at sport. I had plenty of friends and I was careful never to stand out. We had a star system at Alexander Blok, like most schools in Russia at that time, and I quickly became a five-star student or what we called a *pyatiorka*, but I didn't show off about it. I preferred to keep my head down. I got on with most of the staff. In fact, I liked them ... even if Mr Lavrov, the head teacher, used to have such terrible rages that his own head often went bright scarlet.

One of my best friends was a boy called Ilya Platanov. He was two years younger than me so we didn't talk much when we were at school but we lived in the same village and often walked there and back together. Ilya's mother worked in the same factory as my parents, so that was another connection. His father had been a soldier – but he had been killed in Afghanistan. Don't worry – I'm not going to give you a history lesson! You just need to know that the USSR fought a war in that desolate place for ten years, from 1979 to 1989. About fifteen thousand Russian soldiers were killed. Ilya's father was one of them.

For the next few years, things were very difficult for Mrs Platanov. She had enough money to live on – the state gave her a pension and she had her earnings from the factory – but she was very lonely on her own. It was true that she had Ilya and two older daughters – but she missed her husband. She never wore anything but black. If you went to her house, there were photographs of him everywhere.

And then, one day, Igor Krokov limped into her life.

He limped because he too had been badly injured in the war. The story was that he had been a Division Commander with the 5th Guards Motor Rifle Division of the 40th Army in Afghanistan. He had seen action in the assault on the Tajbeg Palace in Kabul until a stray bullet, fired by a Mujahideen resistance fighter, had hit him in the side of his head. That was one story. But there were others who said that he was so unpopular that one of his own men tried to kill him. To this day I cannot tell you which version is true, although I know which one I believe.

In any event, for his part in the campaign he was given a medal: Hero of the Soviet Union. It took the form of a gold star and it was the highest award that a soldier could receive. He was no longer fit to continue in the army so he had become a civil servant, an administrator working for the *duma* – or the city council – of Leningrad. He had many duties. He was a tax collector. He had a seat on the board of the factory where my parents worked. He was a school inspector. I never quite worked him out, to be honest. He was everywhere.

Perhaps you can guess what happened next. Igor Krokov had been in the same regiment as Ilya's father and so it was natural for him to come calling on Mrs Platanov. The first time, he brought flowers. The next time it was expensive chocolates that you could only buy in Moscow. Quite soon, they were spending a lot of time together and about a year later it was suddenly announced that they would be marrying in the village church.

My parents thought it was good news. Krokov seemed to care for Ilya's mother and he could be quite charming if he wanted to be. He laughed a lot, particularly after a few glasses of vodka. Ilya didn't like him though. He didn't trust him and, for that reason, nor did I. There was a look in his eyes that was quite dark and disturbing. It was as if he was planning something and everything he said and did was a lie.

There is one more thing that I must tell you about Krokov. He was not an attractive man. First of all, he was quite short, built like a bulldog with a huge chest and stubby legs. He had a beard which was going grey where it met his ears. But there was something much worse than all that. He had almost died as a result of the gunshot wound (which had also left him blind in one eye) and, after extensive brain surgery, Soviet doctors were only able to save him by implanting a large metal plate in his skull. The hair never grew back there so although he had thick black hair hanging in strands on one side of his head, he was almost bald on the other. I was the one who gave him the name of "Metal Head" and that was what we all called him. Except, of course, for poor Ilya. He had to call him "father".

But here is why I came to hate Igor Krokov and how he did me lasting harm.

He had moved into the house with Mrs Platanov and her three children and quickly became a familiar sight around the village. He tended to wear his old army tunic, which suited his role as a civil servant and reminded everyone that he was a war hero, someone to be respected. He rode a motor-bike with a sidecar attached, although he only carried his own things and never gave anyone a lift. The bike was a Dnepr M-72, the same model that had once been used by the Red Army, although it was well out-of-date and so covered in mud that it was a miracle it worked at all. As I've explained, he worked in the tax office, the factory and at various schools – including mine – and I think it's true to say that everyone was afraid of him.

Imagine a school inspector who can turn up with no warning, who can walk into any classroom, who has complete power over everyone they meet. That was Krokov. He had a gold war medal. He could demand anything and he would be given it. Whenever he came to Alexander Blok, he would be served a huge lunch, with several glasses of vodka, and there would usually be a couple of bottles wait-ing for him as gifts when he left. We children were told to keep well out of his way but to bow our heads if we happened to pass him in the corridor. You could always tell when he was around because the teachers all looked so nervous. He came into my class once and walked up and down the rows of desks and it really was as if a wild animal had somehow crept into the room.

Igor Krokov had a particularly nasty habit. He smoked a pipe and that was bad enough. The cheap tobacco had turned his fingers and teeth quite yellow and had almost certainly done terrible things to his lungs. But when he wasn't smoking the pipe, he liked to hold the stem in one hand and tap the bowl against the plate on the side of his head, so that you could actually hear him approaching from the soft clanging of wood against metal. Even today, I can't hear a bell strike the hour without thinking of Krokov.

A year passed. It's funny how so much time – fifty-two weeks, three hundred and sixty-five days – can be compressed into so few words! But living in a small village where nothing very much ever happened, you never really felt the wheel of time turning. Every day you saw the same people and did more or less the same things. The seasons might move on from one to the next but it was easy to believe that life itself was standing still. It was only if you looked closely that you noticed that, in truth, everything was changing.

Igor Krokov had got fatter. He had a liking for vodka – and he was drinking more and more – but he also enjoyed sticky buns called *kalerikas* – and quite soon he was unable to do up the buttons of his tunic. His wife – Mrs Krokov as she was now – appeared in public less and less. She still worked at the factory and my parents remarked that she looked completely exhausted and, as her husband got bigger, she seemed to be fading away.

I didn't see very much of this – but I certainly noticed that my friend, Ilya, had become a completely different person. When we walked to school together he had been easy and relaxed, always telling jokes, many of them dirty ones. He was somebody you'd call a livewire. But gradually, that all disappeared. He became thoughtful and silent. He didn't laugh so much any more. If you asked him too many questions, he would simply walk away. He never talked about his mother and his stepfather, his life at home, what he did at the weekend. I began to think that he might be ill.

And then the bruises started appearing. One day, he came to school with a black eye. I asked him what had happened and he said that he had hit himself with a cupboard door. But then a few months later it was a series of bruises around his neck. He told me that he'd got into a fight with some of the boys from the village but I knew at once that it wasn't true. He looked haunted. We were walking down a road once and we heard a motorbike approaching. He twisted round and I saw real terror in his eyes.

When did I realize that he was being hurt by his stepfather? Ilya never said anything but I think it became obvious fairly soon. It was almost as if part of him had died. I never saw his sisters, by the way, they were older and hung around with girls their own age. Maybe they were able to look after each other. But Ilya was on his own. Other children began to steer clear of him. They knew something was wrong.

There was nothing I could do to help him, so I

didn't try. In Russia, at that time, every family lived by its own rules and you didn't interfere. I heard my parents talking about Krokov once or twice – and they didn't have anything good to say – but they didn't do anything either. What could they do? You couldn't go to the authorities. Krokov was the authorities. He worked for the *duma*. He could get away with anything.

And then, one day towards the end of the summer, everything changed. It was a Sunday – no school! – and I was walking in the forest, looking for wild mushrooms. It was quite late in the day and I was on my own, some distance from the village, so I was surprised when quite suddenly I heard voices. It was a man talking. I recognized Igor Krokov at once.

"How dare you talk to me that way!" he was saying. "You should be grateful to me."

"Why should I?" That was Ilya. "You're not kind to us. You don't look after us. Since you came into our lives, we've never had one minute's happiness."

"That's no way to speak to your father."

"You're not my father. My father was a good man and you're nothing like him. I hate you!"

I had crept towards the edge of a clearing and I arrived in time to see Krokov looming over Ilya, his face dark with anger. "You should respect me," he warned. There was violence in his voice.

"Why should I respect you? You're a brute!"

"You little swine…!"

Even as I watched, Krokov lashed out. The back of his hand caught Ilya in the face, throwing him off his feet. He crashed down onto a bed of leaves. But that wasn't to be the end of it. Krokov reached down and drew the leather belt out of his trousers, curling one end around his hand. "I'm going to teach you a lesson I should have taught you when I first moved in," he said.

"I'm not afraid of you!"

Krokov lifted the belt and brought the end with the buckle crashing down three times into Ilya's stomach and chest. Ilya cried out, drawing his arms across his face to protect himself. There was nothing else he could do.

I was already moving forward. I was furious. Ilya was half the size of his stepfather. He was two years younger than me. Just a child. And no child should be treated that way ... not ever. I saw a thick branch lying on the forest floor and snatched it up. Krokov was about to hit Ilya a fourth or fifth time. I saw his arm rise into the air.

I was behind him. With all my strength, I brought the branch smashing down onto the back of his neck. Now he was the one who was thrown to the ground, landing on his knees. Ilya looked at me in astonishment, rolling out of the way. Krokov turned round and stared, half in pain, half in anger.

"What the...?" he exclaimed. I will not write here what he actually said.

"Leave him alone!" I shouted.

Ilya had got to his feet. "It's all right, Yasha," he said.

"No, it's not," I replied.

When I had hit Igor Krokov, the branch had broken in half. But a sharp splinter had been left at the end of the piece I was holding. It was shaped like a short spear. I slanted it down towards Krokov's throat and I saw at once that he was afraid. Like all bullies, he was also a coward.

"What do you think you were doing?" I demanded. "How can you behave like that?"

"He's my stepson. This has got nothing to do with you."

"He's my friend. It's got everything to do with me."

"Are you going to use that?" Now he was sneering at me.

I jabbed downwards. The broken end of the stick jabbed into his neck and he squealed. I was only thirteen years old but I was big for my age. I turned to Ilya. "I could kill him," I said. "I could do it for you right now. We could bury him in the forest. Nobody would ever find him. Nobody would know."

Did I mean it? I have no idea. Maybe this was the first indication of what I was going to become. Certainly, looking down at Igor Krokov, who was now close to tears, I felt a wonderful sense of power.

But it wasn't going to happen.

"No," Ilya said. "It's all right, Yasha. Leave him alone."

I pretended to consider. Then, slowly, I lowered the stick. "All right," I said. I turned to Krokov. "But if you ever hurt Ilya again, I will tell everyone what I saw here. Just because you've got a medal, it doesn't mean the police will leave you alone when they discover you've been hurting a child. And I'm not afraid. If Ilya ever comes to school again with a bruise or a cut or anything else, I will find you and I will make you pay. I promise you." I paused. "Ilya, you're coming with me."

"All right, Yasha."

The two of us left together.

You may be wondering how all this prevented me from becoming a helicopter pilot. It is now time to give you the answer. It happened a few weeks later and I will describe it as briefly as I can.

Every year, there was a special exam at the Alexander Blok School. It was terribly important because the three students who got the top marks would be sent to study at a highly respected academy in Leningrad. This was a fantastic opportunity. From a small, provincial town to a major city; from a very ordinary secondary school to a brand new, purpose-built facility with all the latest equipment. This was like becoming a star in Hollywood. It was well known that the boys and girls who went to Leningrad would never look back. They would become leaders. Whatever they wanted to do in their lives, it would happen for them.

I have already mentioned that I was a five-star student and without wanting to sound big-headed, I have to say that everyone in the school knew that I was on my way. My teachers expected it. My parents (who had originally come from Moscow) were thrilled by the idea that I could escape from village life and claim a brilliant future. The other children were all rooting for me. When the exams started, I got about twenty good-luck cards, most of them handmade. We were going to have a huge party when the results were announced. My friends would be sad to see me go but they were happy for me. That was the sort of kids they were.

There were five exams in all. The first four couldn't have gone better. I got exactly the questions I'd been hoping for and I absolutely breezed through the papers. I was feeling fairly confident by the time I arrived at the last exam. It was maths, my best subject. As I walked back into the gymnasium, which had been converted into an exam room for the whole week, I was completely relaxed. I wasn't even particularly worried when I saw Igor Krokov standing at the far end, talking to a couple of my teachers.

I should explain. There was always an independent referee at every exam. By that, I mean someone from outside the school who could check that there was no cheating going on. The teachers at Alexander Blok were so keen for their students to go to Leningrad that it's just possible they might have helped them in some way. The outsider was there to make sure that didn't happen.

Igor Krokov was a school inspector. He was a civil servant. It wasn't really that surprising that he was there.

The exam began at ten o'clock and finished at midday. There were six pages of questions to answer and I finished them easily. They were exactly the sort of questions you would expect: fractions, equations, mathematical diagrams, Pythagoras and so on. I was careful not to be over-confident. Although I finished early, I went through all my work, checking that I hadn't made any stupid mistakes. I won't say I was certain that I'd got everything right, but I was pleased with what I'd done. I knew how much this meant to my parents. I didn't want to disappoint them.

The teacher who was in charge called time. But it was Krokov who came round and collected the papers.

I will never forget the moment he stood in front of me. The last time I had seen him, he had been on his back on the forest bed, gazing up at me with fear in his eyes. Now he was looming over me, in total control.

"Gregorovich," he said, and he managed to put more hate into that single word than I would have thought possible. I handed him my pages. There was a sick feeling in my stomach but at the time I just thought it was the tension of the exam itself and perhaps the loathing I had for him.

What a fool I was! I was not chosen for the academy in Leningrad. It turned out that although I had excelled in the first four exams, I had let myself down badly when it came to my strongest subject, maths. In fact I had only scored sixty per cent.

It didn't seem possible and when the results were put up for everyone to see and the crushing sense of disappointment was still weighing down on my shoulders, I went to the head of the maths department, a woman who had always been kind to me. She looked at me sorrowfully across her desk.

"I'm so sorry, Gregorovich," she said. "I just can't understand it. Why didn't you finish the exam?"

"But I did finish it," I said.

She looked down at her notes. "You're mistaken," she insisted. "You only handed in four pages. Weren't you able to do the others in time?"

"I handed them all in!" I exclaimed.

She shook her head. "You did very well. If you scored sixty per cent, you must have got everything right. If you'd finished the exam, looking at your other results, you'd be on your way to the academy. It's a great shame. It looks as if we're going to be stuck with you for a little while longer."

She was trying to make light of it, but with a terrible, sinking feeling, I knew exactly what had happened. Krokov knew how much the exam meant to me and he had sabotaged my work by stealing two pages of what I had handed in. It had been his revenge for what had happened in the forest. Yes, I could have explained. I could have told everyone the truth. But do you think for a moment that they would have believed me? Of course not! At that moment, I felt a surge of hatred for Krokov that was stronger and more overwhelming than any I had ever felt before or have ever felt since. I wanted to kill him.

I never guessed that one day I would have the chance.

Ten years later, everything in my life had changed. I was no longer living in Russia. Both my parents were dead, killed in an accident at the factory where they had worked. I was twenty-four years old and I had almost nothing in common with the boy who had once attended the red-brick school in Estrov. I do not need to tell my story. All you need to know is that I had been trained by an organization that called itself Scorpia. This stood for Sabotage, Corruption, Intelligence and Assassination. The last of these was my speciality. I had been taught how to use guns and knives and more peculiar weapons too ... crossbows, swords, sickles, ninja fighting fans, different sorts of poison. But actually I did not need any weapon at all. I had learned judo, karate, ninjutsu and many other martial arts. I had been shown more than fifty ways to kill someone in the time it would take to shake hands.

I was not unhappy with the choices I had

made – but perhaps that was part of my training too. There is a difference between murder and assassination. I did not act out of hatred or anger. I didn't know any of the people I killed. They were simply names and photographs that were supplied to me, sometimes with a date when the job had to be done. I was like a soldier in a war. Think about it. If you are told to kill the enemy, do you stop and ask yourself who they are, whether they are married or not, what they are thinking or feeling before you end their life? No, of course not. You simply do what you are told. You might argue that I was not the same, that I was being paid to kill people and that I never acted out of reasons of loyalty or patriotism. But then again, would soldiers join the army if they were not being paid?

At any event, by now I had assassinated about a dozen people, including the Russian businessman who had once imprisoned me, along with his very unpleasant son. The others included several criminals, a handful of corrupt politicians, a major drug dealer and a handful of people whose occupations I never learned. As a result of this, I was already quite wealthy, although I had agreed to give half my earnings to Scorpia in return for the training I had received. I thought this was completely fair.

I had just got back from an assignment in Cape Town when I received my next target, sent to me through a fake eBay account on my computer. This was a clever system. First of all, I had to open the correct website. There I found a second-hand Honda motorbike for sale, available from a dealer in Paris. The bike was in very poor condition and the photograph made it look awful – so no members of the public had been tempted to bid for it. But at exactly twelve noon I entered a bid of my own ... £1,955.45. This was actually a password: 195545. The moment I did this, the bike disappeared and a second window opened up, showing me maps, photographs, diagrams ... everything I needed to know about the man I was going to kill.

His full name was Oskar Fyodor Drozdovski. But that was too much of a mouthful for anyone. He was known simply as Skar.

Skar was not a pleasant person. Born in the Ukraine, he had become a senior figure in the Russian mafia before he had branched out and started his own criminal organization. He was a weapons dealer, selling everything from machine guns to guided missiles, and on one occasion he had actually started a war in order to sell his products to both sides. To amuse himself, he operated a major pipeline from South America bringing drugs into Europe, and he was also involved in blackmail, extortion and vice. It was uncertain how many people Skar had killed but that was hardly surprising. He had buried some of the bodies and dissolved the others in sulphuric acid. He had homes in New York, London, Hong Kong and Moscow. His collection of cars, including a Bugatti Voiture Noire and an Aston Martin Valkyrie, was said to be worth over a hundred million pounds.

No criminal gets to be as rich or as powerful as this without making enemies, and Skar could have filled a football stadium with people who would have liked to see him dead. I did not know which of them had joined together to pay the two hundred and fifty thousand pounds that my services would demand but that was not my business. I examined the information on my computer screen. Scorpia had done their homework. They had provided me with everything that I needed to know – when, where, how – to kill Skar.

It was not going to be easy and that was reflected in the high price that I was being paid. The man I had just finished off in South Africa had been a low-level businessman who had recently returned from an elephant safari. The fact that he had been hunting and shooting the elephants was completely irrelevant and was not, I think, the reason he had been chosen – but all the same I will admit that it gave me a certain satisfaction to push him off the twenty-sixth floor of the hotel where he had chosen to stay. The murder had cost just one hundred thousand pounds and I had economized by not using a bullet.

Skar was very different. He seldom went outside his homes – which were actually more like fortresses – and when he was moving between them he always travelled in a convoy, surrounded by bodyguards. He used bulletproof cars and private jets that were jammed with sophisticated defence systems. The staff employed to protect him numbered forty people – ex-soldiers and mercenaries – and it amused me to read that he even had a personal food taster. I had worked as a food taster once and all I can say is that it left a nasty taste in my mouth.

He had a second wife in New York and a network of friends in other parts of the world but it would be impossible to get to him through them. They were terrified of him. His first wife had given an interview to a newspaper without his permission and he had instantly dissolved the marriage. Then he had dissolved her. He had no children. When he ate out, the entire restaurant was closed down so that he and his friends would be alone. He took holidays only on private islands. Skar was almost untouchable.

Almost.

It interested me that even though he was undoubtedly very clever and very careful, he still had a weak spot. Did he really think his enemies would not learn about it and use it against him? Or perhaps he was just getting careless as he grew older. He was now forty-nine years old and it would be my job to ensure that he did not make fifty.

His weak spot was the opera. He loved going to Covent Garden in London, to the Metropolitan Opera House in New York, to the Bolshoi Theatre in Moscow. Of course he was extremely careful. He never sat in the stalls or the dress circle. He chose instead a private box where he could surround himself with protection officers who would sit very close to him, forming a human shield. He never told anyone where he was going until a few moments before he arrived. That way, it was impossible to plan an attack on him.

But if there is one truth in life, it is that criminals can never trust anyone. They have too many enemies. They are hated for so many different reasons. There are victims, friends and families of victims, people who fear they are about to become victims. There are business rivals and perhaps worst of all, admirers. The admirers want to be like you and the best way to do that is to get rid of you and take your place. Many great criminals have been killed by their deputies. In a way, it's quite flattering.

Someone in Skar's organization had leaked the information that he was going to be at the Bolshoi Theatre for a performance of *The Queen of Spades* by the Russian composer, Pyotr Ilyich Tchaikovsky. It would be a rare moment when he would be out in public and it would surely be possible for a concealed sniper to fire the single shot that would end his business career and his life. I was to be that sniper. I knew there would be challenges. Smuggling a gun into the theatre itself was out of the question. I would have to shoot him when he came out. But first I would have to spot him in the crowd. Almost certainly, he would be wearing a bulletproof vest under his dinner jacket. He would be surrounded by his entourage. I would only have one chance.

Even so, I was sure I could do it.

The very next day I flew to Moscow, travelling in coach as I always do. I can afford business or even first class but why would I want to draw attention to myself? I checked into a cheap hotel and, dressed like any other tourist visiting Russia's capital, I made my way to the theatre. The Bolshoi is a very beautiful building that dates back to the nineteenth century and I might have been impressed by the main entrance with the sixteen white columns holding up the front portico and the four horses pulling Apollo's chariot above. But I was not impressed. All I could think of was that there were no buildings close by, nowhere I could hide to wait for the performance to end. The front of the theatre faced a wide, empty square. If Skar came out this way, I would be unable to reach him, even with a weapon such as the McMillan TAC-50 sniper rifle which can kill from a distance of two miles. It would be too dark. I would not have enough time to find him.

However, the secret informer inside Skar's world had given us further information. We knew the number of the box where he would be sitting during the performance of *The Queen of Spades*, and looking at a map of the theatre we had pinpointed the nearest exit. Unless he wanted to cross the entire auditorium – which would be a risk in itself – Skar would come out onto Petrovka Ulitsa, a narrow street that ran next to the theatre with a huge department store on the other side. This also made sense as his limousine would be waiting for him there and he would have far less ground to cover – no more than ten steps. It would be a gamble, but I checked with my controller at Scorpia and we agreed that I would take up my position here and wait for him to come out. If for some reason he chose a different exit, coming out on the other side of the building, we would just have to wait for another opportunity.

And so, at six o'clock, I found myself in the TSUM department store, pretending to look at the best clothes, the best jewellery and the best of everything that Moscow had to offer. I had a guitar case across my back. It's funny how often I use musical instrument cases to hide my weapons but in this instance it would work perfectly. People would think that I was a musician with the Bolshoi, perhaps killing an hour before the opera began. But it was not time that I was killing. And the guitar case did not contain a guitar.

It was easy enough to make my way up to the sixth floor of TSUM and then find a service stair that led me to the roof. It took me just five seconds to open the so-called security door. If I had been in charge of the department store – and for that matter the opera house – both heads of security would have been fired and sent to some distant location for re-training. It was a cold evening but dry and cloudless. I was wearing thermal under-clothes which would keep me warm. I was using an FR F2 sniper rifle manufactured by Nexter in France, which had been modified to fit inside the guitar case. I also had a Sagem Sword 3-in-1 Sniper scope which would use thermal imaging to light up my target as if he had stepped out at midday.

Now all I had to do was wait. But waiting in my profession is easy. I had been taught the med-itation techniques that would allow me to relax completely, indifferent to the slow passage of time. You might say that I was as stone cold as the statues on the roof of the Bolshoi.

Although there were street lamps, it became quite dark once the department store had closed. Few people walked down the street. Occasionally I heard snatches of notes from the orchestra perform-ing in the building opposite – but only the very loudest ones. At about ten o'clock I realized that *The Queen of Spades* must be coming to an end. A few taxis had turned up and parked and there were also some private limousines. I recognized the ones with the bulletproof windows and the tyres that couldn't be shot out. These would belong to the VIPs in the audience. They would all want to feel protected – particularly in a country where wealth and power could easily become a fast invitation to death.

Then I heard the slow eruption of applause and the shouts of "Bravo!" and "Encore!" as the performers took their curtain call. I picked up the rifle and looked through the scope, perfectly balancing myself on one knee. *The sniper and his weapon are one.* This was something that had been drummed into me by Scorpia but if you have never killed anyone, it is still difficult to explain. Let me put it like this. The brain calculates, the eye sees, the finger pulls the trigger, the bullet flies, the target is hit, the target dies. These are not separate events. They are an organic whole. That is what it feels like to be an assassin.

The moment that I had been waiting for had arrived. There were at least half a dozen doors along the side of the theatre and they all opened at the same moment and suddenly the audience was pouring out into the street, hundreds of people making for the taxis and the limousines or simply drifting into the night. Many of the men were wearing black tie. We are very formal in Russia – more so than in Europe. The women were in long gowns with jewellery sparkling in the street lights. Moving quickly, but not with any sense of panic, I swept my Sniper scope, searching for my quarry. I knew that Skar would not be difficult to find, assuming he had come out this way. I had seen photographs of him and had committed the details to my memory: the bald head, the flabby cheeks, the squashed-up nose that looked as if it had just been punched.

I found him! There he was at the door. I had almost gone past him because he was surrounded by bodyguards. They were moving in a "cross" formation: one man in front, one behind, one on each side. He was wearing body armour, and the target was small, some distance away and completely obscured. For a brief moment I was annoyed with myself. A grenade launcher would have been more effective. Of course, it might have killed ten or twenty people but would that really matter if Skar was one of them?

He moved to one side and although I could see part of his shoulder, his head was still invisible to me. His car was perhaps ten paces in front of him and I knew I had no more than fifteen seconds to make the kill. I tensed myself, trying to find the right moment, and it was then, just as I edged the scope round to follow him, that it happened. A man had come out of the theatre at the same time as him, dressed in a suit and a loud, striped tie. I recognized him instantly even though it was a million-to-one chance that he should have been there.

It was Metal Head.

Igor Krokov.

There could be no mistaking him. The beard, the barrel chest, the hair that had turned grey but still only covered one side of his head. His eyes were red as if he had been crying. Perhaps the opera had been too emotional for him. But as far as I was concerned, it just made him look more devilish than ever. His jacket was stretched tight over the paunch of his stomach. He seemed to be alone.

Despite myself, I felt a surge of hatred rising up inside me. It is critical for an assassin to remain cold and emotionless at all times but how could I help myself? You never forget the things that are done to you when you are thirteen and I vividly remembered the moment in the exam room when he had taken my maths papers and had uttered my name, knowing that he had the power to destroy my whole life. I saw him in the forest too, laying into Ilya with his belt. I had not seen Ilya or his mother since I had left the village. I doubted that things would have ended well for them.

And right then a terrible thought came into my mind.

Kill him!

Why not? Skar was nothing to me. He was just a job – and anyway I didn't have a clear sight on him. He was too carefully concealed by the group of four men who were being paid to protect him. It would be easy to explain to Scorpia that no opportunity had presented itself and although I knew only too well that they never forgave failure, in this case they would understand.

How then would I explain the death of the civil servant? I could tell them he had stepped in the way at the last moment. He was in fact very close to Skar, almost near enough to touch. And there was nobody obstructing my aim.

I had only five seconds to make up my mind. Both

men were moving away from the theatre, across the pavement and towards the road. I could not see Skar but I knew where he was. I knew I could not hit him with a direct shot. What if I were to shoot Krokov first? The crowd would scatter in panic and that might allow me to get a clear sighting. No. I was kidding myself. As soon as the shot was fired his bodyguards would close in on him like a rugby scrum and bundle him into the car. It was one or the other. But which?

Three seconds. The car door was open. The two of them were already moving apart.

Still no clear sight of Skar. I couldn't see his face. Despite the cold night air, I felt a trickle of sweat draw a line down the side of my head.

I made my decision. I curved my finger, gently stroking the trigger. I took careful aim. I fired.

The effect was immediate, like dropping a stone into a bucket of water. Even before they knew what had happened, the entire crowd seemed to ripple outwards. At the very last moment, it was Igor Krokov whose head had filled my Sniper scope and the bullet had blown him off his feet, sending him spinning backwards. People began to scream. A short distance away, the bodyguards had frozen. As professional as they were, they were paralysed, for a brief few seconds, looking for the enemy, wondering where the next bullet might come from.

I turned the Sniper scope back on them and watched them as they came to the terrible realization of what had just happened. Skar was still standing in the middle of them. Even he seemed unaware that he had just been killed. He had been hit in the neck and there was a trail of blood leading down, soaking into the white collar of his shirt. As I watched, he tried to take another step forward but both his legs caved in beneath him. He collapsed and lay still.

Although he had been my target, it had been impossible to shoot him while he was surrounded and I couldn't even see him. I had thought I would have to give up. But then I had realized that there was another way. Making an instant calculation, I had adjusted my aim and shot Krokov, aiming for the thick metal plate that Soviet surgeons had used to save his life. I had worked out the angles. The bullet had hit him and then continued its journey, ricocheting off the metal and travelling sideways into Oskar Fyodor Drozdovski's neck. Metal Head was hurt badly, knocked unconscious. But he would live. The mafia boss, however, was already dead.

As I packed away my equipment and left the roof of the department store, I was happy. I had accomplished my task, my employers would be satisfied and I would receive the full payment for my work. At the same time, I realized now that Krokov was nothing to me. I would have gained nothing by killing him.

I just hoped I'd given him a headache which would last him the rest of his life.

THE WHITE
CARNATION

I have never forgotten a single assignment. There is a special intimacy between killers and the people they kill and sometimes I think I almost owe it to my victims not to forget. Some of them have died bravely, some in tears. Many of them were completely unaware of me and were dead before they knew what had happened. A few have tried to bribe me, offering huge sums of money – four or five times my original fee – to spare them. Of course, I have never been tempted. It is not just a question of my reputation. I would hate anyone to think that I can be so easily bought, which may sound strange coming from a professional assassin but that's how it is. I am true to my word.

I remember. Whether it is the bullet, the knife, or at close quarters with my own bare hands, each death has a special place in my memory. You could say there is an entire graveyard in my thoughts. But there is one incident I remember above all others.

I cannot go to Rome without thinking of it. If I happen to pass a flower shop and see a white carnation, I am reminded of it. It is not good for someone in my profession to carry memories. It is better to keep my head clear for what lies ahead. But this is something I would not wish to lose. I don't know why. But it is important to me.

I was in Rome. I had come to this beautiful city with its seven hills, its classical ruins, its magnificent churches and its superb restaurants because I had been paid to kill a woman I had never met. I had been contacted through my usual network of cut-outs. These were people throughout Europe and America who knew how to reach me but who did not know who I was or what I looked like. These were the days before the Internet when I had to be extremely careful how I was contacted and by whom. Technology has made my work so much simpler ... these days murder comes at the touch of a mouse. Most of my cut-outs were minor criminals who received a small amount of money every month. I am proud of the fact that only one of them ever tried to betray me to the police. I buried him close to the service station at Newport Pagnell although I cannot confirm that he was actually dead at the time.

In any event, I had received an envelope containing a slip of paper with a rendezvous: Room fifty-six, The Hotel Majestic in the Via Veneto in Rome. Nine o'clock in the morning, three days from now. My contact would be booked in under the name of Monica Peretti. The envelope also contained confirmation that the sum of twenty-five thousand euros – the first twenty-five per cent of my fee – had been paid into my account with the European Finance Group in Geneva. I was actually in Zürich at the time, having just finished another job, and it would only be a short hop to Rome. I decided to take the train. I never much liked air travel – and this was long before airports were crammed full of the X-ray machines and metal detectors that make life so difficult for someone like me.

I had a flat in Rome. In fact, by this time, I had flats in almost a dozen major cities, all of them rented under false names. The flat was in the Via Flaminia, a short distance from the city centre near the Villa Borghese, and although it was small and plain, I loved the view over the parkland, the little balcony and the cool breezes in the height of summer. I was also quite fond of the DSR-1 German manufactured bolt-action rifle that I had purchased on my last visit and which lay concealed beneath the floorboards. I was looking forward to using it again.

At exactly nine o'clock, I knocked on the door of number fifty-six. In fact, I had already been at the hotel for three hours. I had eaten breakfast there ... delicious pastries and a cup of very strong espresso. I had sat in the lobby, reading a copy of *La Stampa*. I had wandered through the corridors as if I was looking for someone. And all the time I had been checking that I was not being watched, that everything was normal, that I had not just walked into a trap.

"Come in..." It was a woman's voice. She had spoken in English.

The door was already unlocked. I walked into a suite that would have cost its occupant at least five hundred euros a night. The furniture was antique, the bed king-sized, the curtains sweeping down as if they covered a theatrical stage rather than a window. There was a woman sitting at a desk with her legs crossed. She was about thirty years old, simply dressed, with a string of pearls around her neck and I thought at once that she was the most beautiful woman I had ever seen.

Oh yes, there had been others. Julia Rothman had made an extraordinary impression on me when I first met her in Venice. I had rubbed shoulders with famous actresses and even supermodels. But this woman had something that all the others lacked. The French call it *tristesse*. She wasn't exactly sad, but there was something about her that made you feel sad when you saw her, even before she spoke. She had black hair which fell over her shoulders, slender arms, a long neck. Everything about her was somehow fragile. Her face was so beautiful that it could have been lifted from the pages of any beauty magazine. Blue eyes? Yes. White teeth? Yes. Perfect skin? Of course. I wondered what she was doing here, alone in this hotel room. I wondered who she wanted me to kill.

I did not speak to her. First, I took out a device that resembled a travel alarm clock and flicked a switch in the side. I glanced at the display. It told me that we were not being recorded and that there were no other types of surveillance devices in operation inside or outside the room. Without asking permission, I went into the bathroom, then checked the cupboards and under the bed. This may sound ridiculous, but if you rely too heavily on technology you can forget that there are more old-fashioned ways to listen in on a conversation.

The woman had watched me with amusement. "I see you are a careful man, Mr Forbes," she said. She spoke with an Italian accent. "I like that."

That was the identity I was using for this job. Daniel Forbes. I had a credit card, a passport, a driving licence, a complete life in that name.

"How can I help you, Miss Peretti?" I asked. Her name was quite possibly as false as the one that I was using but I did not think so. I had already confirmed that she had used it to check in, and that there was a Monica Peretti with an account at the Banca Credito Italiano in Rome. My instinct told me that she had not tried to disguise herself and that was interesting. She did not care if I knew who she was.

"I am told that you are the best at what you do," she said. "That you always succeed. You are extremely expensive. Is it true?"

"I am reliable."

"There is someone that I want you to kill." She half smiled as if she had somehow managed to surprise herself but the sadness I had felt when I came in still lingered. "There! I have said it. I have actually put it into words. Now, if you were a policeman, I suppose you could arrest me."

"I am not a policeman. Who do you want me to kill?"

She paused. "My sister." She looked straight at me. "Does that shock you?"

"No, *signora*. I am not easily shocked."

"I suppose not." She paused. "Do you want to know why I am asking you to do this?"

"Only if you wish to tell me."

"Because I hate her. I have always hated her." Something flashed in her eyes. "Even when we were little girls she made my life miserable. She bullied me. She made things up about me. But that's not the reason. Three years ago I married, and I thought that at last I had found happiness. I was in love. I really was. And do you know what has happened? My husband has left me! He's left me for her! My sister has stolen him from me and I have decided that enough is enough. We will never be happy while we are on the same planet so now one of us must leave it. Can you do this, Mr Forbes? Will you do this for me?"

I shrugged. "The reason is unimportant, *signorina*. Do you have the rest of the money?"

She reached out and opened a slim leather

attaché case. The locks clicked loudly as they disengaged. She lifted the lid and I saw the brand new fifty euro notes in their neat bundles, stacked together.

"What is your sister's name? Where can I find her?"

"You do not need to know her name and finding her will be easy. I have arranged to meet her this afternoon on the Spanish Steps."

"This afternoon is too soon. I need at least twenty-four hours to make my arrangements."

She considered what I had said. "That is not a problem. I can telephone her. We can change the meeting until tomorrow. Shall we say four o'clock?"

"Can you tell me what she looks like? Better still, do you have a photograph of her I can take?"

"You do not need a photograph. Nor do I need to describe her. The fact is – she is my twin!" She smiled at me. "Now I see that I have surprised you, Mr Forbes, no matter what you say. We are twin sisters. We look almost identical except that her hair is a little shorter than mine and she wears glasses. You will have no difficulty spotting her. She will be wearing a dark suit with a white carnation in her lapel."

"How can you know that?"

"My sister works as the senior manager of the Hotel Condotti and it's her uniform. It's what she always wears."

"And how can you be sure that she will come if you ask her?"

"It is my sister who has arranged this meeting with me. She wants to pay me off ... to avoid any difficulties. That is the sort of person she is. She thinks that for a few euros, I will disappear from her life. But that's not how it's going to be Mr Forbes. I don't need her money." She waved a hand in the direction of the briefcase. "You can see for yourself. I'm a rich woman. Take the money – and do what I ask."

"Whatever you say *signora*."

In fact, it would normally have taken me a great deal longer than twenty-four hours to set up a kill. It is not just a question of finding the right vantage point from which to take out your target. What is even more important – what is vital – is to ensure that you have your escape route planned. How long will it take the police to surround the building? How many stairways are there, how many emergency exits, how many different streets leading away? If you do not know the answer to these questions, you are dead.

But even as I set about making my preparations, I was aware that I wasn't being as careful as usual. Everything was happening very quickly. There was something about Monica Peretti that made me keen to do as she wished even though I knew that there was something wrong. I could not put my finger on it but it was there, in the air. When you have been working for as long as me, you develop a sense for these things.

I went to the Spanish Steps. There are one hundred and thirty-five of them, with wide terraces, pilasters and great tubs of flowers, rising from the Piazza di Spagna to the church of Trinità dei Monti. They are one of the city's most famous sights. As usual, the steps were crowded with tourists, sitting in the blazing sunshine, strolling up and down, taking photographs of each other. I walked around the area and quickly found what I was looking for. Just opposite was a half-empty office block with access to a flat roof. Better still, the roof connected with two others. The door that led in from the street was old with a lock that would take me less than ten seconds to pick. Climb a few flights of stairs, and I would have the whole of the Spanish Steps in front of me.

On the day of the killing, I crossed Rome carrying my sniper rifle and six rounds of ammunition in a cello case. It was as if I were a member of an orchestra on my way to a rehearsal. I know I must have looked ridiculous, like something from a comedy film, but it's not easy to carry an assault weapon across a crowded city. The truth is, I would have preferred almost any other location. Somewhere quieter. Somewhere less central.

I arrived at the steps at one o'clock when the sun was at its hottest and when most Romans were searching for the inside of a shady restaurant for lunch or going home to enjoy a siesta. I looked around me, then quickly unlocked the door that I had marked out the day before. It opened into a shabby hallway with a flight of steps directly ahead. Nobody saw me. A few minutes later I was lying on the roof with my cello case beside me, out of sight from the street. It was three hours before my victim was due to arrive. Fortunately there was a canopy which provided me with shade.

I took my time preparing my weapon. I had of course already checked the trigger mechanism, the suppressor and all the other moving parts. I unfolded the bipod and made sure that the gun was properly balanced, with the stock fitting snug against my shoulder. I loaded it with the .338 Lapua Magnum bullets I had brought with me. One would be enough. I had no intention of firing wildly into a crowd of holidaymakers. Lying flat on the warm tarmac, I looked through the optical sights (fully multi-coated, manufactured by Lynx in Japan, nitrogen-filled to prevent fogging). I could see everything that moved on the Spanish Steps – the individual petals of the flowers, fluttering in the breeze, the ticking hands of a watch on a tourist's wrist, the hairs on the back of an Italian policeman's neck as he strolled up the steps, completely unaware of what was about to happen.

The woman appeared a few moments before four o'clock. She was dressed exactly as Monica Peretti had said she would be – in a black suit, with black leather shoes, carrying a leather handbag and with a white carnation in her buttonhole. Her hair was shorter than her sister's and styled differently, pinned back. Otherwise, the two women were remarkably similar. Put them on either side of a glass window and you would take it for a reflection in a mirror.

Emptying my mind, I allowed my sights to settle on the flower. At the same time, my finger curled round the trigger. This was the moment that I knew so well. There was always that sense of perfection. The contract was sealed. In one explosive second, life would become death. The white petals filled my vision. If I fired now, the bullet would travel through the carnation and straight into her heart. The woman was standing still, almost as if she was waiting for her death. She was alone. She did not seem to be looking for her sister. She did not move.

And still I had that sense that something was wrong.

I lifted the barrel, allowing the Sniper scope to travel up. I saw the pulse beating in the woman's neck. I saw her lips, her nose and finally her eyes. She was wearing glasses just as I had been told ... and that was what gave her away. It was such a tiny detail. It should have meant nothing. But it is part of my training. I never miss anything. It is one of the reasons why I'm still alive.

Her clothes were expensive.

The shoes were expensive.

The handbag was expensive.

But the glasses were cheap. You could have bought them in any chemist shop for just a few euros, off-the-peg.

I made my decision. Nobody was going to die today. I unloaded and disassembled the DSR-1, then repacked it in the cello case. I made my way back down to ground level and took a taxi to my flat on the Via Flaminia. Nobody noticed me. Nobody said anything apart from the taxi driver who asked me which orchestra I played for.

"Camerata de' Bardi," I told him. It was the orchestra of the University of Pavia and it was actually performing in Rome.

The driver did not ask any more questions, which was just as well. For him.

That evening I returned to the Hotel Majestic and knocked once again on the door of number fifty-six. I was not sure that Monica Peretti would still be there and I was both surprised and pleased when I heard her voice asking me to come in.

She was packing, about to leave, the wardrobes open and her clothes spread out on the bed. She herself was wearing a coat and a headscarf. If I had come half an hour later she would have been gone. She saw me, standing in the doorway, and stopped what she was doing. She closed the lid of her suitcase and turned to me. "Why are you here?" she demanded.

"I did not do as you asked me," I said.

"I know that. You told me this morning that you were reliable. Why did you lie to me?"

"And why did you lie to me, *signora*? Or perhaps it would be simpler if I asked you another question. Why did you want me to kill you?"

I had already seen what I had known would be there. It was on the bed, next to the suitcase. The white carnation. Monica Peretti had been wearing it that afternoon when she had stood on the Spanish Steps. She had pinned it to herself as a target.

She did not reply, so I continued. "You do not have a sister. After I left you yesterday morning, you changed your hair and your clothes. You bought cheap glasses to change your face. You paid me one hundred thousand euros to kill a woman who did not exist. You wanted me to kill you. Why?"

Her lip curled. "It's none of your damned business."

"It is very much my business, *signora*. You used me. I want to know the reason."

"Because I want to die."

Her voice was heavy and suddenly there were tears in her eyes. "I am not going to explain myself to you, Mr Forbes. Why should I? I just have no wish to continue my life and I chose the fastest, the most painless – and frankly the most expensive way to rid myself of it. For some reason, you decided not to fire the bullet. That makes you a failure and a thief. But now you can get out of here. I don't want to see you again."

"I never fail," I said. "And I am not a thief."
I was carrying the attaché case she had given me
and I placed it on the desk. "Here is your money
back. I have kept the twenty-five per cent deposit
to cover my expenses coming here to Rome. But as
for the rest of it, it's yours."

I turned to leave, but stopped at the door.

"I have killed a lot of people who deserved to
die, *signora*. I have killed people who had simply
made enemies. You could say that I know a great
deal about death...

"So let me tell you this. Whatever your prob-
lems, however unhappy you are, you are stupid.
You have beauty. You have money. That alone
makes you better off than half the world. But even
if you had neither of these things, how could you
not wish to see what tomorrow brings? How could
you not want to feel the warmth of the sun on your
skin, to eat ice cream in the Piazza Navona, to
watch the children throwing coins into the foun-
tain? When you came to me, you invited a monster
into your life but if you paid me ten times what is
in that briefcase, I would not do as you ask. There
is no tunnel so long that it does not have light at
the end. I would suggest you find it."

I left her.

I do not know what became of her. I do not know
if she lived or died. But when I remember all the
people that I killed, I think of the one woman I may

have saved and hope that she learned something from our encounter and that she still, sometimes, thinks of me.

WORLD
BOOK
DAY

SHARE A STORY

Well **hello** there! We are

Overjoyed that you have **joined our celebration** of

Reading books and **sharing stories,** because we

Love bringing **books** to you.

Did you know, we are a **charity** dedicated to celebrating the

Brilliance of **reading for pleasure** for everyone, everywhere?

Our mission is to help you discover **brand new stories** and

Open your mind to exciting **new worlds** and **characters,** from

Kings and **queens** to **wizards** and **pirates** to **animals** and **adventurers** and so many more. We couldn't

Do it without all the amazing **authors** and **illustrators,** **booksellers** and **bookshops, publishers,** schools and **libraries** out there –

And most importantly, we couldn't do it all without . . .

YOU!

On your bookmarks, get set, READ!
Happy Reading. Happy World Book Day.

ILLUSTRATED BY Rob Biddulph

WORLD BOOK DAY

SHARE A STORY

From breakfast to bedtime, there's always time to discover and share stories together. You can . . .

1 TAKE A TRIP to your LOCAL BOOKSHOP

Brimming with brilliant books and helpful booksellers to share awesome reading recommendations, you can also enjoy booky events with your favourite authors and illustrators.

 FIND YOUR LOCAL BOOKSHOP: booksellers.org.uk/ bookshopsearch

2 JOIN your LOCAL LIBRARY

That wonderful place where the hugest selection of books you could ever want to read awaits – and you can borrow them for FREE! Plus expert advice and fantastic free family reading events.

 FIND YOUR LOCAL LIBRARY: gov.uk/local-library -services/

3 CHECK OUT the WORLD BOOK DAY WEBSITE

Looking for reading tips, advice and inspiration? There is so much for you to discover at **worldbookday.com**, packed with fun activities, games, downloads, podcasts, videos, competitions and all the latest new books galore.

SPONSORED BY

NATIONAL BOOK tokens

AUTHOR Rob Biddulph

Celebrate stories. Love reading.

World Book Day is a registered charity funded by publishers and booksellers in the UK & Ireland.

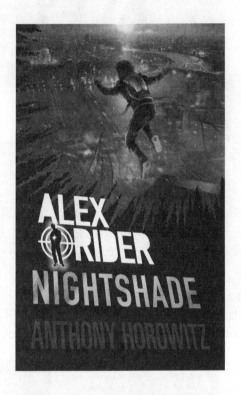

COMING APRIL 2020

**NIGHTSHADE IS COMING.
AND ALEX IS ALONE.**

"EXPLOSIVE, THRILLING, ACTION-PACKED –
MEET ALEX RIDER." GUARDIAN

Alex Rider – you're
never too young
to die…

Alex Rider has 90
minutes to save
the world.

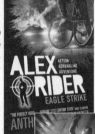

High in the Alps,
death waits for
Alex Rider…

Once stung, twice as
deadly. Alex Rider
wants revenge.

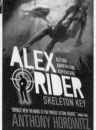

Sharks. Assassins.
Nuclear bombs.
Alex Rider's in
deep water.

He's back –
and this time
there are no limits.

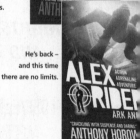

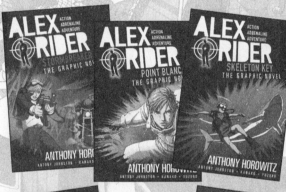
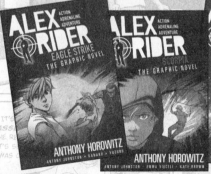

WELCOME TO THE DARK SIDE OF
ANTHONY HOROWITZ

THE POWER OF FIVE

BOOK ONE

He always knew he was different.
First there were the dreams.
Then the deaths began.

BOOK TWO

It began with Raven's Gate.
But it's not over yet. Once again
the enemy is stirring.

BOOK THREE

Darkness covers the earth.
The Old Ones have returned.
The battle must begin.

BOOK FOUR

An ancient evil is unleashed.
Five have the power to defeat it.
But one of them has been taken.

BOOK FIVE

Five Gatekeepers.
One chance to save mankind.
Chaos beckons. Oblivion awaits.

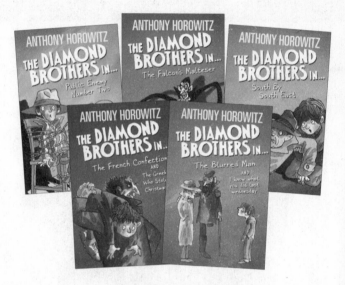

READ MORE WICKEDLY FUNNY ANTHONY HOROWITZ BOOKS

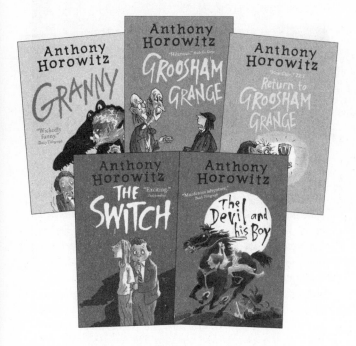

"Move over Roald Dahl, here comes Anthony Horowitz." *Young Telegraph*

"Hugely popular... I can hear Horowitz fans drooling." *The Times*

Photograph © Jon Cartwright

Anthony Horowitz is the author of the number one bestselling Alex Rider books and the Power of Five series. He enjoys huge international acclaim as a writer for both children and adults. After the success of his first James Bond novel, *Trigger Mortis*, he was invited back by the Ian Fleming Estate to write a second, *Forever and a Day*. His latest crime novel, *The Sentence is Death*, featuring Detective Daniel Hawthorne, was a bestseller. Anthony has won numerous awards, including the Bookseller Association/Nielsen Author of the Year Award, the Children's Book of the Year Award at the British Book Awards, and the Red House Children's Book Award. He has also created and written many major television series, including *Collision*, *New Blood* and the BAFTA-winning *Foyle's War*. He lives in London with his wife, two sons and his dog, Boss.

You can find out more about Anthony and his work at:
www.alexrider.com
@AnthonyHorowitz